A Switch Before Christmas

KAREN MCQUESTION

NIGHTSKY PRESS

Text copyright © 2024 by Karen McQuestion

ISBN: 979-8-9870600-6-3

Titles by Karen McQuestion

BOOKS FOR ADULTS

A Scattered Life

Easily Amused

The Long Way Home

Hello Love

Half a Heart

Good Man, Dalton

Missing Her More

Dovetail

The Moonlight Child

214 Palmer Street

A Limited Run

CHRISTMAS NOVELLAS

Wish Upon a Christmas Star

A Time-Travel Christmas

FOR YOUNG ADULTS

Favorite

Life on Hold

From a Distant Star

THE EDGEWOOD SERIES

Edgewood (Book 1)

Wanderlust (Book 2)

Absolution (Book 3)

Revelation (Book 4)

FOR KIDS

Celia and the Fairies

Secrets of the Magic Ring

Grimm House

Prince and Popper

FOR WRITERS

Write That Novel!

AS K. J. YOUNG

The Dark Hour

For Greg, always and forever

Chapter One

Truth be told, Jane Shaw was not looking forward to Christmas this year. Most families had been struggling financially ever since the beginning of the Depression, but Christmas at the Sheridan Girls' Home in 1935 was another thing entirely. No presents of course, but there would be small treats and a change of routine. Of the fifty girls at the home, twenty-year-old Jane was in charge of half of them. Every child at the home worked for her keep, and as one of the lead girls, for her, every minute of every day was full of chores. When her small charges were in school, she cooked, cleaned, and did laundry until her hands were nearly raw.

At night, after seeing them all to bed, she was so tired that her own sleep came quickly and the morning arrived in a blink. That was her usual routine, but Christmas changed everything. This year, the matron, Mrs. Irving, had taken a week off to visit her sister in

Minneapolis. With her absence, Jane and the other lead girl, Mary, had added responsibilities.

The next two days were going to be very trying.

Later that morning, Mr. and Mrs. Sheridan, their benefactors, were coming for their annual Christmas Eve visit. An inspection of sorts, to make sure their money had been well spent.

"You girls must be on your best behavior," Jane had told them. Wearing their uniforms, their hair neatly braided in two plaits, one might think they all looked the same, but to Jane, each one was as different as a snowflake.

"And then they'll give us candy canes?" little Dorothy piped up.

Jane nodded. "Very often they do bring candy, but you mustn't ask, and you should not talk at all unless you're spoken to."

"Except when we greet them, right?" Dorothy asked.

"That's correct."

"Maybe they'll bring Santa with them and he'll have a sack full of gifts," Frances said, her voice tinged with hope.

"Santa doesn't visit orphans," Ruth said, giving her a poke. Jane had learned to keep an eye on Ruth. She'd been sleeping in the streets before someone brought her to the home, and upon her arrival she'd acted as unpredictable and wild as a stray cat. Even now, years later, bad behavior sometimes bubbled to the surface.

"I'm not an orphan," Frances said, sticking out her lip in defiance. "I have a mother."

It was true. Only about half of the girls were orphans. The rest of them had become residents of the home because of some sort of family despair. The actual reason didn't matter. Whether it was money, death, or sickness, the truth of it was that their parents couldn't or wouldn't take care of them.

Jane still remembered her own arrival when she was six. Her mother had taken ill with influenza and died two months earlier. She had no memory of her father, who'd taken off long before, supposedly to find work out west, but he never came back or sent money. He was just gone. None of her relatives had the wherewithal for one more mouth to feed, so it was off to the home in rural Newtonville, Wisconsin. "You'll love it there," Aunt Gladys had said. "Lots of girls to play with and miles and miles of woods."

When the bus had dropped her off and she'd walked from the stop to the home, the sight of the brick building had filled her with awe. Inside, it was a different story. The tile floors, plain furniture, and white walls made the place feel cold and austere, and she felt like an outsider. Even though the staff had been kind and the other girls welcoming, she'd cried herself to sleep for the first week. Eventually, she did make friends and became used to the routine. Before long, the communal lavatories and group bedrooms felt like home. Her aunt regularly wrote letters at first, but after she married and had children of her own, those missives dwindled to birthday cards and Christmas greetings. When Jane graduated from high school, she'd stayed on at the Sheridan Girls' Home as a matter of practicality. She'd had no place to go and no job prospects. Luckily, she had an affection for these little girls and enjoyed caring for them.

Frances, who most decidedly was not an orphan, directed her next question to Jane. "My mother *is* coming to see me the day after Christmas, isn't she, Miss Shaw?"

"Yes, she is." Jane gave the little girl a smile. Frances's mother worked at the mill and lived in a boardinghouse. The family who ran the boardinghouse did not allow children.

Dorothy's smile faded. "I wish someone would come to visit me."

"We'll have lots of fun here," Jane promised. "Hot chocolate and singing carols. And if everyone is good during the inspection today, I'll tell you the Christmas story at bedtime tonight." The girls perked up at this news. Jane had a knack for telling stories that kept them enthralled, and the telling of the Christmas story had become a tradition.

"I can't wait for Christmas," Frances said, her eyes shining. "It's the best time of the year."

Chapter Two

A LOUD BANGING ON her bedroom door awakened Jacquelyn Sheridan. A most unwelcome sound, since she was in the midst of a wonderful dream. In her mind, she was attending an elegant ball and was just about to dance with a handsome stranger. He extended his hand to her, and she was just about to accept his invitation when she heard her brother, David, yelling, "Jacquelyn Sheridan, you answer me right now or I'm coming in there!"

She jolted awake. For a moment, she was confused, and it took everything she had to realize that David was outside in the hallway. Annoyed, she called out, "What do you want?"

"You need to get up and get dressed."

"No." She burrowed under the covers and pulled the sheet over her head. Getting up would happen eventually, but on her own terms. There was no one to tell her otherwise. Their parents were in Europe for the holiday season, and nearly all the servants were off the premises, supposedly at home spending the week with their own families. Not what she would have allowed, but no one asked for her opinion on the matter. Her older brother, David, was the last thorn in her side, but he had no authority over her hours of sleep. If the rest of the mansion was the world, her bed was her own personal island and she was the queen. "Go away, David. Leave me alone."

She heard the double doors leading into her bedroom fly open and David's footsteps as he came into her room. Jacquelyn cringed. She could have sworn she'd locked those doors. She certainly would in the future.

"Get up," he said, standing over her. "You need to get dressed right away or you'll be late."

"Late for what?" She gave him a glare over the edge of the sheet.

"For the Christmas visit at the girls' home."

"Mother and Father do that."

"They're not here, and Mother left specific instructions for you to go in their place." He stared down at her, his face serious. At twenty-three, David had embraced adulthood and all the responsibilities that came with it. Despite the early hour, his appearance was impeccable, as usual. David was handsome, with dark wavy hair and deep-set eyes. His physique was outstanding as well; he was tall and naturally slender with broad shoulders. All of Jacquelyn's friends flirted with him, but he rarely took the bait, calling them "vacuous."

David was an odd one, so different from his sister. The state of the world bothered him. Jacquelyn was so tired of hearing about how the country was going through a depression. As far as she was concerned, the financial troubles of the multitudes hadn't changed their lives much at all. She didn't understand why he was taking on the worries of others, people they'd never met and never would. There would always be soup kitchens, struggles, hunger, and sickness, but none of it was their doing. David was just being silly and overwrought when it wasn't necessary at all. She'd known since she was a little girl that life was meant to be enjoyed. David had yet to learn this particular truth.

"Mother didn't say anything to me."

"Yes, she did, and she included it in the instructions she left behind." He held up a piece of paper.

Through sleep-filled eyes, Jacquelyn recognized her mother's handwriting. Vaguely, she recalled hearing her mother talking about visiting the home in their absence. She hated the idea, so she'd dismissed it, of course, and then promptly forgot all about it. She sighed. "When do we have to go?"

"Not *we*, you. She wants you to start taking on some of the family responsibilities. The foundation is supposed to be run by both of us." It was so like David to remind her of her duties.

The foundation he referred to was the Frank and Irene Sheridan Foundation, a charity established by their parents to create a lasting legacy. Her father in particular took great delight in seeing their names on signs and plaques. It was important to him that others knew of their generosity, and Jacquelyn agreed with this. What good was it to give away money if it went unnoticed?

When David had graduated from university, he'd taken on the role of running the foundation. At the same time, Jacquelyn had somehow been duped into becoming second in charge. Not a job she wanted, but since they'd given it to her, she reluctantly went to the meetings and weighed in on the decisions. And it was a good thing too. Left up to David, the family fortune would be a piggy bank for those who weren't nearly as smart about money. Luckily, he needed her vote of approval to move forward on most expenditures, and she was not nearly as inclined to dole out funds for the undeserving. At their last meeting, David had thrown up his hands and called her stingy. It was a point of contention between them.

Jacquelyn sat up in bed. "So I have to go by myself?"

David exhaled in exasperation. "Yes, because I'm going to be doing another foundation visit elsewhere at the same time. Don't worry, it's really nothing. You walk through, get the tour, and ask the little girls some questions so they know you care. At the end, you hand out the candy canes. It's easy."

Questions? She pictured them as little street urchins clutching at her clothing with grimy hands. What kind of questions could she possibly have for them? She shuddered at the thought. Every fiber of her being dreaded this visit. If it weren't for the fact that it was a direct order from her mother, the holder of her purse strings, she would have refused to go. "All right. I'll do it."

"Good. Eddie is going to drive you. You're leaving in forty-five minutes."

"Forty-five minutes?" She breathed out an objection. "I can't be ready that quickly. It takes more time than that to do my hair!"

"Nobody cares how you look," he said. "Pin it back and put on a hat. You'll be fine."

***

An hour later, she found Eddie waiting for her at the bottom of the stairs. "Don't say a word about me being late," she said with a shake of her finger. "I went as quickly as I could."

Eddie gave her an impish grin. "You look very nice."

Eddie wasn't technically a servant. He was the son of their housekeeper, Mildred, and a little younger than David. Growing up, Eddie and David had been inseparable, the best of friends despite the vast difference in their social standing. Their appearance was opposite as well. Eddie was fair with sandy hair and blue eyes. He was a few inches shorter than David and had nondescript facial features. As far as Jacquelyn was concerned, he was nothing special in the looks department. Right now Eddie was home from university for the holidays. His last year. Usually, he made himself useful when he was back, so at least he wasn't a complete burden.

Once seated on the back seat of the automobile, a warm blanket tucked around her lap, Jacquelyn was happy to find that Mildred had put together a breakfast basket for her to eat on the way. As Eddie drove down the long drive, she nibbled on a biscuit spread with jam. "How long is the drive?"

"About an hour."

"And then an hour back again?"

"That's generally how it works." Eddie sounded amused.

This was going to take up her entire day. "Ugh. This is so tedious. It's my Christmas holiday too. I shouldn't have all these endless chores." Technically, it was only the one chore, but it still felt like too much.

Checking her coat pockets, she found her custom-made leather gloves. They'd come in handy after she was done eating. She could have kicked David for rushing her this morning. In her haste, she'd forgotten her handbag, which was a shame because she wouldn't be able to check her appearance and powder her nose right before arriving. Chances were good that the guttersnipes at the orphanage wouldn't even care, but what if she were going somewhere important? Her brother should have given her more notice.

They left their enclave near the lake and drove through the city, an area Jacquelyn always avoided. The streets in the vicinity were dotted with garbage, and the homes and businesses were ramshackle in appearance. Why would anyone let their house get so run-down? No pride at all. Why, with a little paint and some repairs, these places wouldn't be nearly as disgraceful. And so few Christmas decorations! If anyone had taken the time to string up some garland or hang a wreath, it would have gone a long way toward making things seem more festive. Honestly, these folks were lacking in common sense.

"It's a cold day to be standing in line," Eddie said as they drove past a line of men standing gloomily along the sidewalk.

"Why don't they go inside?" she asked.

"They're waiting to go inside. It's the rescue mission."

"Oh. So they're like me. Waiting to get somewhere. Endless waiting."

"I've driven your parents to the girls' home the last few years," Eddie said. "I think you'll find it of interest. There's a young lady in charge of the little girls who looks exactly like you."

Jacquelyn sat up straight. "You're joking!"

"No, I'm not. Exact same auburn hair and green eyes. About as tall. She could be your twin. Didn't your parents ever comment on it?"

"No. I would have remembered such a thing."

"She's nearly identical in looks to you. Her name is Jane. I noticed her right away."

"I'm quite sure she doesn't look like me," she said indignantly. Eddie had spent much of his childhood teasing her, and now she was certain he was doing it again. "I don't believe it."

"You'll see for yourself once we get there."

"Hmmm." Jacquelyn finished the biscuit. "Maybe we should just drive in silence for the rest of the trip. I think a quiet ride would be best."

"If that will make you happy, that's what we'll do." His tone was still teasing, but she didn't care. As long as he obeyed, she could tolerate some occasional insolence.

Chapter Three

THERE WAS SO MUCH to do that morning that Jane barely had time to catch her breath. Breakfast cleanup came first, then making sure all the girls were presentable for the Sheridan visit. She inspected their fingernails and the backs of their necks, spots that often were missed during their twice-a-week baths. Their hair was checked as well, to make sure that all of the plaits were tightly braided, no strands out of place. Mary, her counterpart, did the same with her small charges.

As Jane walked through the home, she was filled with a sense of pride. A Christmas tree in the entryway was festooned with ornaments created out of salt dough. The paper chains the girls had made earlier in the week were now draped over each doorway and window. They'd used donated newspapers and magazines, which had stained their little hands, but the ink had washed off with laundry soap and a bit of scrubbing. The girls were proud of their efforts, and Jane was pleased to have thought of these activities since it had kept them all busy and resulted in brightening up the place.

When she was done with the preparations, Jane was glad to see that every room and hallway looked clean and festive.

While Mary gathered the girls together to practice the Christmas songs they'd sing for Mr. and Mrs. Sheridan, Jane took the opportunity to freshen up. In the bathroom, she leaned over and stared into the mirror over the sink, critically assessing her appearance. For so many years her auburn-colored hair had been parted in the middle and braided, just like the rest of the girls.

As an adult, her style had not changed that much. She still braided it, but now it was in one long braid, wrapped around her head and pinned in place. Mary had once commented that Jane's hair had a natural curl. "If you set it at night in pin curls, you could wear it loose and in waves. You'd look like a movie star," she'd said, her head tilted to one side. Jane liked the idea, but there never seemed to be extra time in the day to fuss with her appearance.

Now, she checked her hairpins to make sure her braid was securely fastened around the crown of her head, then splashed a little water on her cheeks and forehead. After dabbing her face with a towel, she took a step back, smiled, and checked her teeth. Clean and presentable. As long as none of the girls misbehaved, the Sheridan visit should go well.

Mary and Jane lined the girls up in the front hall, half on either side. The Sheridans, usually so punctual, were late this time around, so Mary kept the children occupied by playing a game of Simon Says while Jane stood guard by the door, watching for the automobile to pull into the drive. When she spotted the dark vehicle making the turn and heading toward them, she called out, "They're here! Everyone, take your places!"

As the girls shuffled into two straight lines, Mary gave them a last-minute pep talk. "Backs straight, face forward. Do not speak unless you're spoken to first, then use your best manners." Jane gave Mary a nod, then slipped out the front door to greet the Sheridans. She and Mary had flipped a coin to see which of them would have the honor. She'd won, but now, in retrospect, she wished she hadn't.

The matron had always done this in the past, waiting outside and then ushering the grand couple indoors while regaling them with stories about the children. The anecdotes were designed to assure the wealthy husband and wife that their money was well spent and that these girls would grow up to be good citizens, a credit to the home. Jane, suddenly shy and tongue-tied, did not feel up to taking the matron's place. At least she had her introductory sentence memorized.

She'd mentally practiced the words before she'd fallen asleep the night before: *Welcome, Mr. and Mrs. Sheridan. I'm Jane Shaw, taking the place of Mrs. Irving, who unfortunately could not be here today. We're so pleased to have you visit us this holiday season.*

Mary had assured her that everything after that would come easily. "They're just people like us," she'd said. "The matron says they're always very nice to her. Pretend they're like anyone else."

Now Jane stood outside the front door, back straight, face forward, her hands clasped together. Without a winter coat, she felt the full force of the December wind. A slight shiver came over her as powdery snow drifted down, dusting her shoulders and the top of her head. The sleek black vehicle came to a stop. The driver, a young man with sandy blond hair, came out of the vehicle and trotted around to the other side, giving Jane a friendly smile as he went. He opened the door, and to Jane's surprise, only one person exited, a young woman wearing a cherry-red wool coat with an ermine collar and a matching red hat with a medallion of fur on the brim.

Hurriedly, Jane came down the steps. Her welcome speech, which had been on the tip of her tongue, slipped away at the sight of this unexpected person. *Where are Mr. and Mrs. Sheridan?* As her right foot hit the bottom step, it skidded on a patch of ice, knocking her off balance. As her feet came out from under her, she made a split-second decision. Grabbing the young woman's arm, her only chance of staying upright, was not an option, so she fell to the brick pavement at the bottom of the steps, landing on her knees. The impact knocked her breath out. The driver rushed to her side and held out a hand, which she gratefully accepted. Shakily, she got to her feet. Facing the young lady who'd just exited the vehicle, she found herself looking into a familiar set of green eyes.

The elegantly dressed young woman narrowed that same set of eyes and turned to the driver. "Don't tell me this is the girl you think looks like me?" She raised a haughty eyebrow.

"One and the same." The young man's voice was chipper. "Spitting image."

"You couldn't be more wrong." Now the young woman sounded angry. "She looks nothing like me."

"If you say so," he said with a laugh.

Jane brushed off the front of her dress, which was now damp and ripped. She held out her hand. "Welcome to the Sheridan Girls' Home," she said. "Whom do I have the pleasure of meeting?"

Chapter Four

Jacquelyn sighed. First Eddie thought this girl looked like her, which was totally outrageous, and now this clumsy pale copy didn't even recognize her? How often had her picture been printed in the society pages of the local newspapers? So many times that she barely noticed anymore, except to complain if she'd been photographed from an unflattering angle. Everyone knew Jacquelyn Sheridan, from the maître d' at every restaurant in the city to the student body at every private school she'd ever attended. Salesgirls rushed to help her as soon as she walked into their establishments. At the foundation offices, the two secretaries fawned over her as if she were a movie star.

So how was it that this girl couldn't place Jacquelyn? She shook her head and frowned, then reluctantly took her hand and gave it a quick squeeze. "I am Jacquelyn Sheridan."

"Welcome, Miss Sheridan. I'm Jane Shaw." Jane Shaw's brow furrowed as she spoke, as if she was puzzled.

Jacquelyn spoke primly. "It's nice to meet you." The wind kicked up, sending gusts of snow swirling around them, but Jane Shaw appeared shell-shocked and unable to move beyond the present moment. Well, it was clearly up to Jacquelyn to run this show. "Shall we go inside?" Without waiting for a response, she walked past the awkward girl and up the steps. Jane followed mutely, while Eddie scrambled up ahead to get the door.

Walking into the building, Jacquelyn was greeted by a wall of girls on either side of the hallway. They wore identical gray dresses, some sort of sackcloth-inspired fashion.

"Girls," Jane said, "please welcome Miss Sheridan to our home."

After a slight pause, they spoke in singsong unison. "Welcome, Miss Sheridan." The sound of their voices echoed off the walls. One of the littlest girls repeated it after the others had finished.

"My apologies for the delivery. We were expecting Mr. and Mrs. Sheridan," Jane said. "We practiced it that way."

If they expected to hear details of the Sheridan family's personal life, they were going to be sorely disappointed. "My parents had other obligations," Jacquelyn said. "So I offered to go in their stead."

"I see."

Jacquelyn scanned the two rows of children. They weren't the grimy ragamuffins she'd envisioned, thankfully. At the very least, they were clean and orderly. "What are we waiting for?"

A young woman with dark brown hair stepped forward. "Mr. and Mrs. Sheridan usually like to interact with the girls before we start the tour." She gave Jacquelyn a respectful nod. "I'm Mary Howard. Jane and I are the lead girls here. Mrs. Irving left us in charge while she is away. May I take your coat?"

Jacquelyn shook her head. "I won't be staying that long. I understand there's an inspection, and then I'll be on my way."

Eddie spoke up. "Excuse me, Miss Sheridan, but your parents always hand out candy canes before they leave."

The girls murmured in excitement, and Mary sharply reprimanded them. "Girls, silence please. Remember your manners."

Eddie said, "Would you like me to go out and bring in the candy?"

Jacquelyn waved a hand to indicate she didn't care either way. A minute ago, she hadn't even remembered that there would be candy canes, and now she was expected to decide how they'd be distributed? "Eddie, it's inconsequential. Do as you like," she said.

One of the girls raised her hand high in the air.

"We aren't speaking, remember, Agatha?" Mary said.

Agatha bounced on her toes, about to burst with excitement. "But the fancy lady looks just like Miss Shaw!" The other girls nodded in agreement and whispered to each other.

Not this again. Jacquelyn gave Jane a careful look. Same color hair and eyes. About the same height and build. Her facial shape was identical, and yet Jacquelyn didn't see the resemblance. Her own face was angles and high cheekbones, the visage of a movie star, while Jane's face was softer, less refined. At a distance, they could be mistaken, but a twin? No. Anyone who said that wasn't looking closely enough.

"Quiet, girls," Mary said, a finger to her lips. "At the Sheridan Girls' Home, we are polite and only speak when spoken to." A hush fell over the group.

Jane spoke up. "Girls, why don't you go with Miss Howard to the dining room while I show Miss Sheridan around?"

Mary motioned for them to follow her, and the girls silently walked away.

Jacquelyn was glad to see them go. Time to get this over with and return home.

Jane said, "If you'll follow me, Miss Sheridan, I'd be pleased to show you how your family's generosity has changed the lives of all the girls who live here."

Chapter Five

It was unnerving to see someone who was the mirror image of herself. Jane found herself avoiding a direct gaze as she moved forward with the tour, searching for things to say as they walked through the building. "You've already seen the entryway. Over here is Mrs. Irving's office. She's the matron in charge here." Jane led the way into the room.

Mrs. Irving's desk was neat, holding a black Royal typewriter, a telephone, a desk lamp, an empty jam jar filled with pencils, and a framed photo of her late husband. Jane had never seen the surface of the desk devoid of paperwork until now. Presumably, everything had been tucked away in the filing cabinet or desk drawers. A framed painting of a bowl of fruit hung between two windows. "I'm guessing that Mrs. Irving keeps in touch with the foundation during the year and speaks to your parents, but I don't know for certain how that works."

"My brother and I head up the foundation." Miss Sheridan's tone was imperious. "Not my parents."

"I see." Jane lingered next to the desk, not sure what to say next.

Miss Sheridan took off her gloves and stuck them in her pockets. "Well, let's get going, shall we?"

Sensing impatience, Jane walked more quickly, narrating as they went. She showed her the working area of the kitchen and the shelves filled with food supplies.

"It seems very well stocked," Miss Sheridan observed with one raised eyebrow. "No one goes hungry, I assume?"

"No, Miss Sheridan, no one here ever goes hungry. Because of your family's generosity, every child here has what she needs to grow up to be healthy, educated, well mannered, and proper." This was a line Jane had heard the matron utter many times.

"Very good." Miss Sheridan nodded approvingly.

Jane opened the swinging door to show the girls seated at the tables in the dining room, their heads bowed in prayer. How clever of Mary to have found an activity to keep them quiet. "I think it would be best not to disturb them."

"I would agree with that."

Jane led her to the area they called the gathering room. It was spacious with a brick fireplace and bookshelves. Two large davenports sat on opposite walls. Wooden tables with straight-backed chairs filled the middle of the room. This room was used for studying or smaller gatherings. Sometimes on winter nights when the girls had gone to sleep and a fire was burning bright in the fireplace, Jane slipped into the room and pretended this was a library in her own house. It was the kind of room a wealthy family might have, the kind dreams were made of. "The older girls use this room for studying and writing papers. It's also in use if the girls get visits from family."

"Family visits?" Miss Sheridan said. "I thought they were orphans."

"Many of them are, but about half have families who can't care for them." Jane remembered one father who'd shown up roaring drunk, stumbling and shouting. Mrs. Irving had to send him away. The little girl had been waiting for her daddy's visit for weeks. When she found out what had happened, she'd sobbed for hours.

"Why, that's preposterous!" Miss Sheridan frowned. "Their families refuse to accept their responsibilities? I don't agree with parents refusing to shoulder the burden of raising their own children. It's laziness."

"Many of the parents are sick or lacking funds to pay for food and education," Jane said gently. "For most of the girls, the Sheridan Girls' Home is their only chance to have a secure, happy childhood. We're all grateful for the kindness and generosity of your family."

"I just don't approve."

Jane tried again. "My own mother died when I was a little girl. My father had gone missing years before, and my relatives couldn't take me in. Without this place, I don't know what would have happened to me. The home fulfills a valuable role, especially now with the Depression. The Sheridan name has become synonymous with the improvement of society."

Miss Sheridan's expression softened. "Everyone knows that it's my family who pays all the bills here?"

"Yes, the girls pray for your family's health and happiness every night. And the people in the village also know that Frank and Irene Sheridan and their foundation are the founders and benefactors of this home. Your family is famous for their benevolence."

"Well, that's something, anyway."

Jane gestured toward the hallway. "Shall we proceed?"

As they walked, Miss Sheridan asked, "Where are the classrooms?"

"The girls attend class in the village. It's about a mile walk from here." She turned into one of the sleeping rooms. "This is one of four sleeping quarters for the girls. Mary and I also sleep in the same area as the girls, so we're available if they have a bad dream or become ill during the night. Mrs. Irving has her own room." Before them was an expansive room with rows of cots. At the end of each cot was a trunk labeled with the last name of a girl. Everything each girl owned had to fit in her trunk, no exceptions.

Miss Sheridan walked through the room, reaching down at one point to press on a mattress. With a bewildered look on her face, she turned to Jane. "Where do they keep their pillows?"

Jane shook her head. "We don't have pillows here."

"Why not?"

"It's an unnecessary luxury. We have all that's needed and nothing more. Each girl is assigned a set of sheets and two blankets, one light blanket and one heavy one. The heavy one is made of wool. It goes on top."

Miss Sheridan nodded in what looked like approval. After a long pause, she asked, "What's next?"

"The lavatory, I guess." Jane led the way to the communal lavatory used by her group of girls. The one used by Mary's charges was on the other side of the hallway and was identical to this one. Once inside, she gestured to the tubs, the partitioned toilets, and the trough sink topped with a long mirror. "It's set up to accommodate the fact that many girls use it at the same time. We have twice-weekly baths with warm water." This was a point of pride at the home. Other facilities bathed less often and in cold water. Or at least that's what she'd been told.

Miss Sheridan walked into the middle of the room, taking it all in. She stopped in front of the mirror, looking at herself and then Jane. "Can you believe that people say we look alike?"

She'd sounded so offended that Jane wasn't sure what to say.

Miss Sheridan stepped closer to the mirror and stared, then adjusted her hat before looking back at Jane. "If they think it's a joke, I don't find it funny."

"It's probably because our hair is the same color."

"Hmmm." Miss Sheridan folded her arms and gave Jane a long look. A smile crossed her face. "You know what would be hysterical? If we switched clothing, just for giggles."

"Switch clothing?"

"Yes!" Miss Sheridan sounded gleeful. "We should switch clothing and fix your hair to match my own. I can even braid mine to look like you." She shuddered. "I bet it would take all of ten seconds before the difference becomes apparent. Eddie for sure would be able to tell us apart instantly. So much for us looking identical. I would be the one to have the last laugh."

"That would be one way to prove a point, Miss Sheridan," Jane said. "But it's a bit drastic, don't you think?"

"No," she said with a grin. "I don't think it's drastic at all. It might turn out to be the most interesting thing that's happened to me all week."

Chapter Six

Fifteen minutes later, they stood side by side, surveying their collective appearance in the mirror. For Jane, the switch had been complicated by the fact that Miss Sheridan had more undergarments and hairpins than she'd anticipated. On Miss Sheridan's part, she obviously found pulling on Jane's clothing distasteful. "It's like wearing a burlap sack," she'd declared, buttoning up the front of the dress. "How can you stand it? Personally, I would never tolerate such a thing."

Now, fully attired and hair fixed, the resemblance was astounding, something Jane found both odd and enthralling. The sensation of wearing luxurious well-fitting clothing was something she'd never experienced. The fabric felt smooth to her fingers. The red coat cinched at the waist, highlighting her slim silhouette. The ermine collar was soft against her neck, and the matching hat, tilted ever so slightly, brought the look together. Jane had never thought much of her looks, but now, seeing herself like this, she almost felt beautiful. She couldn't even imagine how much this ensemble cost, but she knew she might never have the opportunity to dress like this ever again.

Miss Sheridan rubbed her hands together. "All right. Listen carefully and do exactly as I tell you."

"Yes, Miss Sheridan."

"We'll go out and I'll speak to your people and pretend to be you. Then we'll go find Eddie in the entryway, and you can tell him you're ready to go home." Her face widened in a grin. "Do not come back until he recognizes that it's not me."

"What if he doesn't?" Jane was having trouble differentiating between the two images in the mirror herself. Depending on how observant Eddie was, there was a definite possibility that he might not notice.

"He will. I want him to admit he was wrong, so just keep playing along until he does. I am going to make him eat his words."

"I hope you're right."

"I *am* right," she said with more confidence than Jane had ever had. "If he won't admit defeat, you'll need to call his bluff and keep acting the part of Miss Jacquelyn Sheridan. No matter what, do not give in. Do you understand?"

"Yes, I understand," Jane said.

"Now tell me what I should say to your people. If I'm going to play the part, I want to get this right."

By the time they walked out of the lavatory, Miss Sheridan had practiced her lines several times, adding hand gestures that weren't quite Jane's style, not that she was going to say as much. The Sheridans put food in her mouth and a roof over her head. Criticizing one of her patrons was never an option.

Miss Sheridan walked ahead of Jane into the dining room, where the girls were still assembled. "Girls, Miss Sheridan needs to leave soon," she said, motioning to Jane. "So she only has time to listen to one Christmas song. Make it a good one."

The disappointment at only being able to sing one song showed on the girls' faces. They'd practiced for days. Mary rose to the occasion and smoothly said, "Of course." She directed the girls to get up from the tables and cluster together in a semicircle. Once they were in position, she turned to Jane. "Miss Sheridan, we would love to perform 'Angels We Have Heard on High' for your listening pleasure. We hope you enjoy it." Mary raised her hands and motioned for them to begin.

Listening to the girls sing made Jane's heart swell with gladness. She was so proud of how they came together as a group, no fidgeting or pushing, their posture perfect while their voices filled the room with Christmas cheer. She knew every one of the girls and was familiar with the stories that had led them to the home. Every single one had experienced hard times, unfair difficulties, and sadness, and yet they still found reasons to be grateful and happy. When they finished, they looked at Jane expectantly, reminding her that they needed Miss Sheridan's acknowledgment.

Jane clapped. "That was beautiful, girls. I'm so proud of all of you for coming together to create such heartwarming music in the true spirit of Christmas. All your practice paid off. You sang like angels." She suspected that this was not what Jacquelyn Sheridan would have said, so she waited for one of them—Mary, Frances, Ruth, or any of the other girls—to recognize her, but no one said a word. The girls just beamed at her compliments.

Miss Sheridan acting as Jane said, "Say goodbye, girls. Miss Sheridan has to make the long ride home."

"Goodbye, goodbye," they called out.

Frances added, "Thank you for coming to see us." Even though the little girl had spoken out of turn, Jane couldn't help but feel pleased at her kind words.

As Jane and Miss Sheridan walked out of the room, Jane heard one of the girls say, "But what about the candy canes?" Behind them, Jane heard Mary shush the child.

In the hallway, Miss Sheridan said to Jane, "I guess I'm not surprised that mere children couldn't figure out our ruse. Simpletons. Eddie will spot the difference immediately."

Eddie was waiting in the front entryway, a paper bag at his feet. His face lit up as they walked into view. "Did you have a good visit?" he asked.

Jane, realizing he was speaking to her, said, "Yes, I did, Eddie. I just need to hand out the candy canes and then we'll be finished."

"Very good." He handed her the bag. "I'll be waiting right here for you. Unless you want me to go out and warm up the engine."

"No," Miss Sheridan said. "Wait for her here."

Retracing her steps, Jane found the girls, still together in the dining room. "Who wants a candy cane?" she asked, holding up the bag.

As expected, the room filled with the sounds of fifty voices calling out, "I do! I do!"

"Use your manners, girls," Mary admonished.

A chorus of the word "please" came next.

Jane gave them out, one at a time, happy that each of them remembered to say thank you. "You girls have the best manners," she said. Glancing over at Mary, she tried to catch her eye and bring her in on the joke of the switch, but Mary remained serious and polite. "Have a very Merry Christmas," Jane said and waved goodbye before leaving the room.

She and Mary would have such a good laugh tonight when she told her the whole story of switching clothes in the lavatory. She couldn't wait to tell her all about it.

Chapter Seven

As Jane walked away with the bag of candy canes, Jacquelyn watched her critically, thinking that her movements did not match the fine clothes on her back. Jacquelyn had always prided herself on moving gracefully, while Jane's strides were brisk and no-nonsense. The contrast between the two was as plain as the nose on her face. Everyone had to see it. The residents of the home were either complete dullards or too timid to point out the obvious switch. Eddie, however, was another matter. He'd known her for her entire life. Jacquelyn stood out from the crowd, she always had, and Eddie was no idiot. He knew.

She found Jane's clothes to be shapeless. The dress was made of stiff material that didn't complement her movements. It was just there, hanging off her body. The rip and the dirt stains at knee level, the result of Jane's tumble down the stairs, made Jacquelyn feel unwashed. Jane's stockings sagged, wrinkling around her ankles.

Even Jacquelyn's childhood playclothes had more style than this, and they were certainly more comfortable.

There was no way Eddie couldn't tell that she didn't belong in this place, in this set of clothing. He was being stubborn in not acknowledging that she and Jane had traded places. Waiting in the lobby with him was the perfect opportunity to jab at him a bit. She would get him to give it up. After this was over, they'd have a good laugh on the way home and then again when she told David what she'd done. Growing up, the boys had enjoyed playing pranks on her and on each other. She'd show them that she was every bit as clever as they were.

For a few minutes, she and Eddie waited quietly in the lobby. Finally, she stepped closer and spoke. "So," she said, "do you enjoy your job working for the Sheridans?"

"Very much so, thank you."

This was not the response she'd expected. She tried again. "Do you know who I am?"

"Of course. Miss Jane Shaw. Mrs. Irving says that you're a tireless worker and the girls love you." He gave her a warm smile.

What? He'd been talking with the matron about the help here at the home? Jacquelyn wondered when this had happened. She answered carefully, remembering her role in this particular theatrical production. "I do my best. It's not an easy job. I work morning, noon, and night." This last comment was designed to make him laugh and then admit that he knew it was Jacquelyn. She suspected he might tease her and say he'd known it was her because she'd never worked a full day in her life, something that was mostly true.

"I imagine it is difficult," he said thoughtfully. "But I admire how kind and patient you are with these girls."

"Thank you."

Off in the distance, they heard the girls' voices thanking Jane for the candy canes. Jacquelyn said, "It's very kind of the Sheridans to provide these girls with a home and treats for Christmas. They must be wonderful people." If that didn't break through his façade, she wasn't sure what would. She waited for him to say, *Oh come on, Jacquelyn. Enough with the playacting. I've known it was you the whole time.*

Instead, a pensive look came over him. "I can't say a bad word about them. They took my mother and me in when I was little. I can't remember a time before living with them. They gave my mother a job in her darkest hour and provided us with a place to live and food to eat." He leaned in and lowered his voice. "Not too many people know this, but they're also paying for my university education."

What? Jacquelyn had no idea her family was paying for his schooling. What an outrage. How could this have happened? She knew the money didn't come out of the foundation's funds, so it had to be paid for personally by her parents. Right out of their bank accounts. That money was her future inheritance, and she didn't approve of it being frittered away in that manner. "Really?" She arched one eyebrow. "They pay the entire thing?"

"Yes. Sometimes I still can't believe it. Mr. Sheridan said I had a keen mind and he wanted me to have the chance to fulfill my potential. Believe me, I don't take it for granted. I hope to make them proud."

Besides commenting on her appearance, Jacquelyn had never heard her father compliment her, not even once. Before this, she'd never given her father's opinion of her much thought, but now she wondered why he'd never encouraged her academically. Did he think she was stupid? Lacking in potential? Or maybe it was it because she was a daughter and not a son. Not much was expected of her, that much was true. She'd always found the lack of expectations freeing, but she realized now it was a bit of an insult.

Before she had a chance to find out more, Jane returned to the entryway, still wearing the red coat and hat, the paper bag dangling from one hand. Her appearance startled Jacquelyn. It was like seeing herself from another angle. Maybe they did look a little bit alike.

Eddie straightened, his posture becoming formal. "Are you ready to leave, Miss Sheridan?"

Jane looked unsure. She glanced at Jacquelyn, who gestured to the door. They might as well see this thing through. Jacquelyn said, "Thank you for coming today, Miss Sheridan. So very generous to give us your time. The girls loved seeing you. I know that for me you're a lady I look up to and admire." She shot a glance at Eddie. Certainly this would catch him off guard and make him laugh. But no, there was no reaction. If anything, he looked a little uncomfortable at the lavish praise she'd just bestowed upon this new version of herself.

Eddie said, "Thank you, Miss Shaw." And to Jane, "Shall we go?"

After a quick look in Jacquelyn's direction, Jane answered, "Yes, please." Eddie held the door for her and didn't even look back. He was holding firm to the joke as long as possible, Jacqueline thought. Much as it killed her, in a minute, she would admit defeat.

Chapter Eight

Jane had waited for Miss Sheridan to stop this charade, and when she didn't, she walked outside with the driver, Eddie. That was his name. He'd driven Mr. and Mrs. Sheridan in the past, and she'd thought she'd heard them call him by name. This year she'd listened more carefully and heard Jacquelyn Sheridan confirm it. Young men did not cross her path all that often, so she took note of it. This one was handsome, with neatly parted hair and good manners. He had a kindly countenance as well.

Up close, the black Rolls-Royce was a showstopper, long and sleek. Oh, it would be heaven to sit inside it, even for a minute. Eddie opened the back door for her, and she slid into place. The gray leather upholstery had some give to it, making it a comfortable seat. She set the paper bag on the floor at her feet, careful not to crush the four leftover candy canes. It had occurred to her to leave them with

Mary, but there was no good way to divide them among the group, so she left them in the bag and took them with her.

Eddie closed the door and went around to the other side, getting into the driver's seat. Jane stared out her window, waiting for Miss Sheridan to come bursting out the door, putting an end to this joke. She was starting to feel uncomfortable for having gone along with this, but what choice did she have? Miss Sheridan had insisted and had specifically said she would be the one to say when to quit, that Jane should just play the part until that happened. Feeling her heart begin to race, she exhaled audibly.

Eddie looked over his shoulder. "It's going to be cold for a few minutes. We have to wait for the heat to kick in."

A heater? How fancy. "This is a Rolls-Royce?"

"I know it's a Rolls-Royce." Eddie sounded annoyed. "But you still have to wait for the heat. It doesn't magically show up just because you're cold." He drove away from the building and down the drive.

Jane craned her neck to look back at the home. How far did Miss Sheridan want to take this? She sank back in her seat and took a few breaths. Should she say something? Her heart sank, making a knot in her stomach. Finally, she came out with it. "I'm not who you think I am," she said, her voice raised over the sound of the engine.

Eddie laughed. "Oh, I know who you are. Believe me."

"Really?" Now she was confused.

"Let's not talk anymore. Remember? A quiet ride would be best."

His voice had an edge to it. She had such limited experience dealing with men that she wasn't sure if he was angry or just being formal. One thing was certain: it wasn't her place to contradict him.

Chapter Nine

AFTER THE HEAVY DOOR closed behind them, Jacquelyn frowned. This was not turning out the way she'd expected. Old Eddie had more gumption than she'd given him credit for. He'd turned the tables on her and she never even saw it coming. Well, bully for him. She knew that her brother was going to love hearing about this. She suspected that she'd never live this one down.

Outside, she thought she heard the sound of an automobile door shutting. Eddie probably opened it and closed it to fool her and was grinning like an idiot even now. Getting her clothes back would be the first order of business. She scratched at her neck where the collar had been rubbing. Honestly, what was this cheap dress made of?

Well, two could play at this game. To save face, she'd give Eddie until the count of thirty before she opened the door to check. When she finished counting, she peered outside, shocked to see the back end of the Rolls-Royce as it left the driveway and turned onto the road. "Wait!" she yelled, even knowing there was no way Eddie could hear her at this distance. Inside, she seethed. The nerve. Now he was taking it too far. Jacquelyn was going to have a thing or two to say about Eddie once they got home.

Jacquelyn clutched the edge of the doorframe, her eyes squinting toward the distance. He had to come back. He just had to. Certainly that little fool Jane Shaw had let him in on the joke by now. She stood there waiting until the cold draft was too much, then let the door slam shut and went inside.

This was ridiculous. If he wasn't back in fifteen minutes, she was calling home to demand that David come and get her. Her heart sank when she remembered that David had gone somewhere today and probably wasn't even home right now. *Darn.* Well, no matter. Eddie would be back any minute, and he'd be sorry for putting her through this. She'd have a talk with her father and have him cancel Eddie's tuition payments. Yes, that's what she'd do. Eddie would just have to pay for his own education.

And if he didn't return soon, she'd have someone here drive her home. Then if he turned around and came back, she'd be gone. Maybe he'd worry at having lost his precious passenger. She smiled at the idea of turning the tables on him.

Walking down the hallway, she followed the sounds of the girls chattering in the dining room. She found them sitting at the long tables working on their candy canes, with Mary standing in the middle of the room.

"You're back!" Mary said. "Did Miss Sheridan leave?"

Still keeping up the pretense. Could it be that she really didn't see the difference? Jacquelyn said, "They've gone, but they'll be back."

"Why is that?" Mary's forehead wrinkled.

One of the little girls got up from the table and ran into Jacquelyn, nearly knocking her over, then wrapped her arms around her waist. "Miss Shaw! I'm so excited about Christmas! Are you really going to tell us a story tonight? We were good."

The other girls perked up then, adding their own Christmas comments.

"Yes, a story!"

"Christmas is my favorite time of year."

"And we don't even have to do chores for two whole days!"

Jacquelyn looked down at the little girl's face. She'd actually be cute, given the right clothes. "You need to go sit down," she said, shaking her off. The child, who looked crestfallen, trudged back to her seat.

"They're just so excited," Mary said, making an excuse. "They're looking forward to having hot chocolate."

"I love hot chocolate!" said one of the older girls. All of the others loudly agreed with her.

The noise level was aggravating. Jacquelyn felt the onset of a headache. "I need to talk to you," she called out, beckoning to Mary. When they were close enough to speak quietly, she said, "I'm not Jane Shaw. We switched clothing as a joke. I'm Jacquelyn Sheridan."

Mary burst out laughing. "Jane, you're too much." She gave her a gentle punch in the arm. "Always making merry."

"I'm being completely serious. I thought it would be readily apparent, but it seems I'm surrounded by imbeciles. Now your Miss Shaw seems to have taken off in my car, and I have no way to leave this horrible place."

"You're really Jacquelyn Sheridan?"

"Yes, that's correct."

"I don't understand. Why would you switch clothing?"

Fools and idiots. She wasn't sure which category this young woman fell into, not that it mattered. "The reason is not any of your concern. All that's important is that I need your help in getting home. Do you drive?"

Mary shook her head. "No, I don't."

"I need someone to drive me back to civilization. Is there someone else here who can provide that service? I will pay them, of course."

"Mrs. Irving has the only car, and it's quite a hike into the village. I'm not sure if anyone there would be able to help either."

"You do have a phone, though?"

"Yes," Mary said. "In Mrs. Irving's office. We're not allowed to use it without her permission, though. She's very strict about that rule."

"I have a feeling Mrs. Irving won't mind if I make a call."

Chapter Ten

A MILE DOWN THE road, the car came to the village, driving smoothly past all the familiar places. Since Jane had come to the home, she'd only seen the village when walking to a specific destination, and usually she'd been keeping track of the other girls and not paying attention to the buildings. Driving by was a new experience. Jane pressed her nose against the glass, taking it all in. First came the church, and then there was the school building and adjacent schoolyard. Beyond that was a row of small businesses, including the butcher shop and bakery. Next came the post office.

The Rolls-Royce drove slowly down the middle of the village, attracting attention. Some children having a snowball fight paused to watch it drive by, while others walking on the sidewalk pointed and stared.

On the outer edge of the community, they passed the local tavern, the Mule. She'd never actually ventured that far into the village, but she'd heard all about this place. Prohibition had been over for two years now, and in that time it had developed quite a reputation. One of the newer girls had often gone to the Mule to retrieve her father and had witnessed some terrible things firsthand. She'd regaled the others with stories of fistfights, broken bottles, and men toppling off bar stools. It sounded like an awful place for anyone, much less a child.

Leaving the village, they drove past farm fields, and Jane felt her anxiety melt away. The feeling that she'd done something wrong was still there, lingering in the background, but it was fading with every mile. She'd only done as instructed by Miss Sheridan. Also in her defense? When she'd broached the subject, Eddie claimed to know what was going on. Perhaps this was some kind of Christmas exchange scheme? Unlikely, but then again, the whole thing was bizarre. Swept up in this situation, she felt uneasy. Getting a break from the home for a few hours did have some positives, though. The girls might feel temporarily abandoned, but Mary often left to visit her aunt, while Jane had never had a holiday from the home since the day she'd arrived. This outing might only last another hour or two. Certainly she'd be going back very soon.

On the seat next to her was an empty basket and a small plaid blanket. Jane took the blanket and covered her lap, tucking it in on each side. Her window was frosted on the inside, so she scratched at it with a fingernail, clearing a small opening, then gazed out at the farm fields. "How long is the drive?" she asked.

"Still an hour." She heard Eddie sigh. "Believe me, I'm driving as fast as I can."

"I know you are. Thank you."

He glanced back. "Are you feeling well?"

"Yes, thank you. Why do you ask?"

He shook his head, returning his attention to the front windshield. "Just making sure there's not exhaust coming up through the floorboards."

"Goodness. Does that happen sometimes?"

"It never has before."

"Oh. I see." Rich people could be so confusing.

By the time they reached the city, the heater had done its job. Jane watched in awe, taking in the dense traffic, tall buildings, and crowds of people coming and going along the sidewalks. "What's that up ahead?" she asked when Eddie stopped at an intersection.

"Where?"

"That line of people?" A line of one person after another stretched down the block and around the corner. Most of them were men, but in the back of the line Jane caught sight of a weary woman wearing a man's gray coat with a scarf tied under her chin. She held the hand of a little boy about three or four. Next to her stood two older girls, one of whom didn't have a coat on at all. She wore a dress she appeared to have outgrown, and she hugged herself as if her folded arms would keep her warm.

Eddie said, "It's a soup kitchen. Sometimes they hand out food for folks to take home."

"What kind of food?"

"Canned goods. Occasionally they have bread or vegetables. It varies."

"So these people are hungry?"

"I imagine so. No one would stand out in the cold otherwise."

As Jane watched, the mother of three turned her head, revealing the exhaustion etched on her face. "They all look so miserable."

"That they do. There's a depression going on, in case you hadn't noticed."

Inexplicably, an urge came over Jane. Later, she couldn't quite explain the impulse. At the time, it seemed the only thing to do. "Can you wait, please?" She grabbed the bag of leftover candy canes and the plaid blanket and exited the car. As she slammed the door behind her, she heard Eddie voice an objection, but she didn't stop to find out what he'd said.

She approached the woman and said, "Excuse me, ma'am. May I give your children some candy canes?"

The older girl's expression lit up with joy. "Can we, Mother?"

The mother looked guarded. "I don't have any money."

"I'm not selling them," Jane said. "It's a Christmas gift. I'd like to give them to you."

Her eyes widened. "Well, if they're free, then yes, they would like that very much."

Jane handed each of them a candy cane, including the woman. "Merry Christmas to all of you."

The mother's eyes welled up with tears. "Merry Christmas to you too, miss. You're an angel here on earth. Children, what do we say?"

They responded with a delighted chorus of "Thank you!"

Jane wrapped the plaid blanket around the shoulders of the girl without a coat. "This should help you stay warm."

"Can I keep it?" Her big brown eyes were hopeful.

"Yes, it's yours now. A gift."

The child said, "Oh, thank you! It's so soft."

"You're welcome." She heard cars honking from the street. Eddie hadn't moved, and the vehicle was now blocking traffic. "I have to go now. Merry Christmas!"

"Merry Christmas!" they called out in unison.

She scrambled over the snowy walkway back to the car. As soon as she was safely inside with the door shut, Eddie drove away. A few blocks later, he spoke. "That was very kind of you."

Jane said, "Will it be a problem that I gave away the blanket?" That was her only regret. It hadn't been hers to give, and she didn't have the money to replace it.

"A car blanket? There are a dozen more like it stored in the garage. It won't be missed."

He said the words so casually, and yet, Jane thought, the blanket that wouldn't be missed made all the difference in the world to one cold child.

Chapter Eleven

After Mary gently told the children that they must be on their best behavior or they wouldn't get hot chocolate that evening, she reluctantly led Jacquelyn to Mrs. Irving's office. Along the way, she said, "Maybe your driver and Jane will be back soon, Miss Sheridan. We could wait a while and see. Then you won't need to use the telephone after all?"

Such trepidation, thought Jacquelyn, every word lacking conviction. Mealymouthed, that's what Mary was.

Jacquelyn was good at taking charge, which was good because that was the only way things were going to get done. "I've waited long enough," she said. "I'm not waiting another minute."

"I'm just saying it might not be necessary after all, miss. The telephone is really only for emergencies. We're not supposed to use it."

"Maybe *you're* not supposed to use it, but I'm sure the rules are different where I am concerned."

"You're probably right, miss."

As soon as they walked into the room, Jacquelyn spotted the black telephone on one corner of the desk, the cord trailing to a plug in the wall. She went around to Mrs. Irving's chair, took a seat, and picked up the receiver. It wasn't until she went to dial the operator that she noticed the cylindrical lock fastened between the numbers. "What is this?"

Mary said, "I had heard that Mrs. Irving had a lock made special by the locksmith in the village just recently, but I didn't know she'd locked it before she left. She wanted the girls to know that the telephone is only for emergencies."

"And this is clearly an emergency!" Jacquelyn didn't mean to shout, but it seemed to be the only way to get through to her.

Mary's eyes widened. "I'm sorry, miss. I wish I could help you."

"You *wish* you could help?" Jacquelyn waved her hand dismissively. "If wishes were horses, beggars would ride. If you really want to help, you'll get me the key." She opened the desk drawer and started rifling through the paper clips, typewriter ribbon, pencils, and other detritus.

"It's not in there," Mary said, her voice tremulous. "It's not here at all. Mrs. Irving keeps it with her at all times. I'm sure she took it with her on her holiday."

"Did you not just say the phone is for emergencies?"

"Yes, I did, Miss Sheridan." Mary stepped back as if afraid of being struck.

"So why on God's green earth would she leave all of you here without a working telephone? What if one of the children had a high fever or broke an arm?" The incompetence was galling. This Mrs. Irving needed to be fired and replaced by someone with half a brain.

"You're right, of course. It doesn't make sense. I'm not sure why she took the key," Mary said. "Except that she had a problem once when one of the girls used the phone without permission. Since then, she's kept it locked all the time."

"You tell me. What good is it if you can't use it?"

Mary shrugged. "In an emergency, if we needed the doctor, either Jane or I could walk into town and fetch him."

"Well, that's what you must do, then. I'll stay here, and you go into town and fetch someone to drive me home."

Mary shook her head. "Oh no, miss. I don't really know anyone in town who could do that, and in any case, I can't leave the children."

Jacquelyn's eyes narrowed. "Are you outright refusing my order?" This was something she had never encountered before. Without exception, everyone, from the tailor to her parents to the other girls at school, had always let her have her way. Once, at home, she'd stamped her foot at being denied a new frock, and her father had laughed and said, "I'm so sorry. I forgot for a minute who I was speaking to." After that he'd allowed her to order the dress, never questioning the cost. That was how the world worked for her. Up until now.

"I would love to help you, but it's not possible."

"Of course it's possible. Just do what I tell you to do."

"The good news is that we can still receive calls."

"And how exactly would that help me?"

Mary pursed her lips. "It's so odd to see you dressed as Jane. It's uncanny. You look like her, but you don't act like her."

"I understand that Miss Shaw acts differently. Of course that's the case—she hasn't seen the world like I have. I understand what it takes to get things done. I'm a Sheridan. Do you think my father could have built an empire by meekly sitting back and waiting to see what happens?"

"I would guess not."

"So I'm telling you again that you need to find someone to drive me home. Immediately."

Mary straightened. "Miss Sheridan, my responsibility is to these fifty girls. Now that Jane is gone, it's up to me alone to oversee their health and safety."

"Oh my word." She had no patience for excuses. "I think they can be left for an hour or so. Besides, I'll be here."

"I'm sorry, Miss Sheridan. I can't abandon my responsibilities. The answer is no." Mary turned her back on her and walked out of the room. Just left, as if Jacquelyn was of no consequence at all. Did she not understand that if not for the Sheridan family's generosity she and the rest of the urchins would be out on the street? *The nerve.*

Jacquelyn followed her, calling out, "Then have one of the older girls go instead. The fresh air and exercise would be good for them."

Mary didn't even turn around, just shook her head. Such galling behavior. Mentally, Jacquelyn added Mary's name to the list of those she wanted fired from the Sheridan Girls' Home. *Jane. Mrs. Irving. Mary.* She'd have all three of them packing their bags and out the door before the year was over. There was a depression going on, and people were begging for work. Plenty of people would love to have such an easy job.

She also had to deal with Eddie, who'd driven off and left her behind. *Stupid Eddie.* How could he not tell the difference between herself and Jane Shaw? She was in a terrible predicament. It was hard to say who was at fault, but there was enough blame to go around.

When they reached the entrance to the dining room, Mary stopped to speak with her. "Did you want to tell the girls that you're not Jane, miss, or would you like me to do it?"

Jacquelyn said, "Why should we tell them anything? They're children. It's none of their business."

"They're going to notice the difference," Mary said. "They adore Jane."

Was she implying that Jacquelyn was not the type to be adored? *Such nonsense.* "Listen, I honestly don't care what you do because I won't be here that much longer. Just go about your business. I'll be busy figuring out a way to get home."

"I'll tell them that Miss Shaw is not feeling well and that they shouldn't bother her." Mary cast a nervous look at the girls in the dining room, who were now all curiously watching them.

"Fine. As long as I'm left alone." Why would she care if the girls noticed that Jane was gone? She wasn't here to comfort upset children. It wasn't in her nature. Mentally, she cursed out her brother David. This whole trip had been a mistake—one she'd never make again.

Chapter Twelve

After leaving the downtown section of the city, Eddie drove through a poor neighborhood, the kind Jane remembered from her early years of living with her mother. Neglect showed in the sagging roofs, cluttered porches, and snow-covered walkways. At one home, she saw an old lady peering out a window, holding the curtain back to get a better view of the Rolls-Royce. Even though it was so close to Christmas, there were no signs of Christmas decorations, something that made her sad. Even at the home they'd made an effort to make the holiday a special one.

Turning a corner, Jane caught sight of two little boys making a snow fort. Their cheeks were rosy and they were laughing. The sight confirmed something she'd always believed—that even in the worst of times, a person could find a reason to smile.

Eddie expertly maneuvered around snowdrifts and parked automobiles. As they left that neighborhood and crossed over to the next, the houses became nicer and the yards larger. From there they came to an area of stately manors. In twenty minutes, they had left one world and entered another. Jane took it all in. The homes of the wealthy and the privileged. Some of them were larger than the Sheridan Girls' Home. What would it be like to live in such a place? It would be like living the life of royalty, she decided. Everything grand and clean, with servants to do all the work. Would she get bored living such a life? She didn't think she would.

Eddie broke the silence. "We're in Whitefish Bay now. It won't be much longer."

"Thank you." She idly wondered what would happen once they arrived at their destination. Was he taking her to the Sheridan home? Judging from the other residences, that was likely. She tried to make sense of the fact that Eddie had said he knew exactly who she was and yet he still continued to drive her all this way. There had to be a plan in place, something she didn't know about. The idea made her a little uneasy.

He turned off the main road into a driveway that curved past a rectangular pool with a row of statuary fountains spouting in the center. Snow covered the lawn and the manicured hedges in front of the grandest and most elegant of all the mansions she'd seen that day. "Oh," she breathed, her palm against the glass. A red tile roof topped a two-story building constructed of Cream City brick. Tall columns framed the arched double doorway that served as the entrance, and the glass doors in the second story above it were fronted by a wrought-iron balcony that reminded her of *Romeo and Juliet*. Large Christmas wreaths decorated the double front doors.

"Home again, home again, jiggety jig," Eddie said in a cheery voice as the car came to a halt. He glanced back. "What? You don't have some snide comment about what I just said?"

"No." She was puzzled. "Why would I?"

"No reason."

The Rolls-Royce had stopped but the engine was still running, making her think either she was getting out or someone else was going to be joining them. "So I take it this is my stop?" she questioned, hoping against hope that the answer was yes. If the outside was this impressive, she could only imagine what it looked like on the other side of those doors.

"It is unless you want to be delivered to the garage." He chuckled. "The front door is unlocked. My guess is you'll find Mildred in the kitchen, if you're hungry." He turned and looked back at her. "Do you need me to open the door for you?"

"No, I'll take care of it," she said. "Thank you for the ride, Eddie."

His expression changed to one of amusement. "The mockery is uncalled for, but on the off chance you're being sincere, you're welcome."

"I'm being sincere."

"Well then, you're very welcome."

Jane left the car and went up two steps until she faced the imposing front doors. As Eddie drove away, she glanced back at the rolling lawn and circular driveway with the fountains in the middle. She stood immobile, her hand on the knob for at least a minute. Finally, she mustered up some courage and went inside.

Chapter Thirteen

Jacquelyn backtracked to Mrs. Irving's office, where she took a seat behind the desk and then turned on the desk lamp to better study the lock. A rudimentary design. She should be able to figure this out. She unfolded a paper clip and jammed the end into the lock, wiggling it back and forth, waiting for the click of a release. But the click never came, and eventually she tired of trying. Why had this Mrs. Irving made her phone as impenetrable as a bank vault? *So ridiculous.* She tried another tactic, attempting first to pull the lock off with her bare hands, then hitting it with a stapler.

A little girl lingered in the doorway, watching her. "What are you looking at?" Jacquelyn said. The child's face showed surprise, but she didn't leave, just kept staring with deep-set soulful eyes. Well, let her watch, if that's what she wanted. It was all the same to Jacquelyn.

When hammering the phone with the stapler didn't work, Jacquelyn ran out of ideas. In frustration, she picked up the phone and turned it over, repeatedly slamming it against the desk's leather blotter until the surface became scuffed and dented. When that effort failed, she knocked the blotter to the floor and slammed the phone against the top of the wooden desk, scratching the surface. Finally, she threw the phone on the floor and burst into tears. In despair, she rested her head on her folded arms and cried.

Never had she felt this frustrated and hopeless. She had to be the most miserable creature in the world.

Her tears soaked the sleeve of Jane's dreadful dress, not that Jacquelyn cared. When she was done here, this terrible dress would go straight into the fireplace. She cursed under her breath while imagining the acts of revenge she'd carry out on her brother, Eddie, and the staff here at the home. A lot of people were going to pay for her suffering.

While she sobbed, she felt a small hand stroking her hair. Over and over again, little fingers softly combed over the back of her head, trailing onto the back of her neck. Something about the gesture seemed familiar in a way Jacquelyn couldn't quite place. It felt good to know someone cared.

"Please don't cry." The child's words came in a whisper. "I know you're sad, but things will get better. You're going to be fine."

The little girl kept caressing her hair until finally Jacquelyn lifted her head to take a look. All of the girls at the home had looked the same to her, but now, seeing one close up, she could see beyond the braids and the plain uniform. This dark-haired child had a smattering of freckles across her nose and brown eyes framed by dark lashes. She looked to be about eight years old, and she was offering a handkerchief, which Jacquelyn gratefully accepted. After dabbing her eyes, she asked, "What is your name?"

The little girl giggled. "You know I'm Frances."

"You're a good girl, Frances. How did you know to comfort me?"

"I learned it from you."

"You did?"

"Yes, remember? When I first came here? I used to cry, and you gave me your handkerchief and told me that change is always hard at first but that things will get better." She smiled. "And then it did get better, and now I almost never cry anymore."

Things will get better. This from a little girl who lived in an orphanage, or at least a place like an orphanage. Jane had apparently fed this child this inane, cheery pabulum. *Well.* Jacquelyn had to begrudgingly admit that a person going through a difficult time might find the words reassuring. "Thank you."

Frances wasn't done. "And tomorrow is Christmas, the best time of the year!"

This child was incredible. She was looking forward to a day that would bring her almost nothing. Jacquelyn said, "I admire your boundless enthusiasm."

"Maybe you should wash your face and rest. That helps sometimes."

Jacquelyn considered the suggestion. It wasn't the worst advice she'd ever heard. She felt a surge of generosity toward little Frances. Later on, when all of this was over and the staff here was fired and replaced by more competent employees, Jacquelyn was going to buy a beautiful doll and have it sent to the little girl. Or maybe she'd come and deliver it herself. The idea made her grin.

Chapter Fourteen

Jane walked into the mansion and stopped, taking it all in. The entryway ceiling was divided into raised sections, with gold medallions decorating each intersecting piece. The floor was constructed of glossy inlaid marble tiles, while an elegant curved staircase led to a landing featuring a large window.

And Christmas? It was everywhere. Garland wrapped the length of the staircase banister, and two Christmas trees were within view, one at the base of the stairs and another on the landing. Blown glass ornaments glimmered in front of the trees' electric lights, and each one was topped with a beautiful angel. She thought ruefully of how proud she'd been of the plain homemade ornaments the girls had made back at the home. No wonder Miss Sheridan hadn't been impressed.

In the past, she had tried to imagine how wealthy people lived, but she could see now that her imaginings had never even come close.

Her vision had come from seeing how Daddy Warbucks lived in the *Little Orphan Annie* comic strip. Seeing it come to life was another thing entirely.

Even as she stood in awe, she was aware her time here was limited. At any moment she was going to be returned to the home, so if she was going to tour the mansion, it was best to do it right away. She could go a lifetime and never have another opportunity to see a house this luxurious. She climbed the stairs, pausing to look at the tree on the landing and then continuing to the second floor.

Jane peered into every room, expecting to find someone, anyone, but all was empty and quiet. One of the rooms had a pastoral scene painted on the ceiling, and others had velvet drapes and statuary on pedestals, as if this were a museum. When she came to a room with women's clothing strewn on the floor, she had a feeling she'd found Jacquelyn's bedroom.

She went inside and looked at the framed photographs that lined the dresser. Each one was a time capture of Jacquelyn Sheridan's privileged life. Most of them had been taken with her parents or brother, posing in various rooms in the mansion. Jane could only imagine such a life.

Next, she paid attention to the clothes lying on the carpet. Mrs. Irving's words, "Always leave a room better than you found it," echoed in her ears. With that in mind, she picked up each item. She set a damp towel aside and placed the clothing on the bed. When done, she assessed the collection. None of them seemed dirty or rumpled. In Jane's world, that meant they could be worn again. She investigated further and found that the doors on one wall led to a spacious bathroom and a closet combined with a changing area. So many clothes, and all for one person!

Jane hung the damp towel on a rack in the bathroom and inspected her reflection in the mirror above the sink. Still wearing the red coat and hat, she felt like she was Jacquelyn Sheridan.

Would she switch lives with Miss Sheridan permanently if she could? She tilted her head and gave it a thought. It would be nice not to have to work so hard and have so little to show for it. And sometimes the commotion of all the girls chattering at once gave her a headache and made it hard to think. Working at the home, it was easy to think her life wasn't leading to anything in particular. She'd always wanted a home of her own, a husband, children, travel. None of that seemed forthcoming in her current life, but that didn't mean that her efforts lacked purpose. She saw the difference she made with the little girls every single day. They loved her and she loved them. It would be hard to walk away from that.

While in the bathroom, she took the opportunity to wash her face and rinse her mouth. Quietly, she got into the large claw-foot tub, careful to drape her feet over the end so as not to scuff the surface. Soaking in a bath this deep would be heaven.

When she left the room, she was startled to see a woman silently putting the clothing on the bed into a wicker laundry basket. The woman, who appeared lost in thought, had hair pulled back into a severe bun and wore a gray dress with a lace collar and a frilly apron. She turned when Jane came into the room and gave her a big smile.

"Oh, there you are! I'm sure you're hungry. I have soup on the stove, if that would please you. Or I can make something else. Just say the word!"

Jane's stomach rumbled. "Soup sounds delicious, thank you. Oh, and Mildred?"

"Yes?"

Such a relief to know that she'd guessed correctly. This was Mildred, the one Eddie had referenced. "I need to tell you that I'm not Miss Sheridan."

"Oh, I know. Eddie told me there was some kind of mix-up at the home."

"I don't know that I'd call it a mix-up." Was the older lady understanding what she was saying? It didn't seem like it, but Jane couldn't think of a way to say it more plainly. "It was not my idea, but we switched clothing to see if anyone would notice. She told me not to say anything until Eddie noticed. I tried—"

Mildred said, "You don't need to explain to me. I make a point to keep my nose out of the family's business. I'm here to do my job."

"I see."

"Just come downstairs when you're ready, and I'll get the soup for you." Mildred headed to the door but stopped just short of leaving. "Why don't you give me your coat and hat?"

Obediently, Jane unbuttoned the coat and shook it off her shoulders, then handed it to Mildred. The hat was a little trickier since it was held in place by a long hatpin. She felt around the crown until she located the jeweled end and successfully pulled it out.

Mildred took the hat, then said, "Shouldn't you insert the hatpin into the brim so they stay together?"

"Of course." That made sense. She reunited the hat with the pin, and Mildred left with a satisfied smile. There was so much to remember here. The complicated undergarments, the extensive wardrobe, and Mildred, who worked for the Sheridans but didn't get involved in anything beyond her own duties.

Jane went into the bathroom to tidy her hair before heading downstairs for soup. Now all she had to do was find the kitchen.

Chapter Fifteen

JACQUELYN, WHO ALWAYS PRIDED herself on taking charge, allowed Frances to take her by the hand and walk her down the hallway to the sleeping area. Along the way, they encountered other girls milling about. "Miss Shaw is going to take a nap, so we have to be quiet," Frances told them. This simple statement apparently qualified as news at the Sheridan Girls' Home, as the words spread down the hall.

"Miss Shaw is taking a nap!"

"Shhh, everyone. Miss Shaw doesn't feel well."

"We have to be quiet."

As she and Frances walked, other girls followed, until there was a small crowd accompanying them.

Jacquelyn freshened up in the lavatory, unpinning the braid and raking through her hair with her fingers until it fell loose around her shoulders. When she came out, she found Frances and about a dozen other girls standing by a bed. A bed that she guessed to be Jane's. Sleeping on this narrow mattress wasn't appealing, but Jacquelyn wasn't going to argue. She'd never felt so spent in her entire life. Every ounce of energy gone. Obediently she crawled under the covers. "No pillow?" she asked, forgetting what Jane had told her.

"We don't have pillows here," Frances said, as if this would be obvious.

One of the girls took off her sweater and rolled it up, then offered it to her. "Sometimes when I want to put my head on something, I use this," she said.

Jacquelyn lifted her head and let the girl tuck the rolled sweater underneath. It wasn't perfect, but it helped. "Thank you." Jacquelyn closed her eyes. "Frances, could you tell Mary to come and get me when the car comes back? Can you do that?"

"Yes, Miss Shaw. I'll tell her."

As she slipped into sleep, she felt small fingers stroke her hair, and she remembered why this gesture seemed familiar. It was exactly what Mildred had done when she was a small child. So comforting.

Chapter Sixteen

As Jane sat at the kitchen table eating soup, Eddie got himself a bowl from Mildred, who ladled it from the pot on the stove, then took a seat across from her. "Enjoying your lunch, Miss Shaw?" he asked.

"Very much so, thank you." The soup was a hearty chicken noodle served with sourdough bread. Mildred had wanted to seat her in the dining room, but she'd insisted on eating in the kitchen instead. She'd only had to look at the formal table for twelve situated underneath a crystal chandelier to know that it wasn't the place for her. Now, sitting in the utilitarian kitchen across from Eddie, she was relieved to hear him use her name. It made her feel better knowing she wasn't purposely being deceptive. She dabbed her mouth with a napkin. "So you knew I wasn't Miss Sheridan the whole time?"

"Not the whole time." He shook a napkin with a flourish and lowered it to his lap. "I had a bit of a feeling as we were driving. You were very polite, for one thing, but what really clinched it was when you got out of the car to give those children the candy canes. That was very kind of you."

Something about the way he smiled made her blush. "It was a small thing," she said. "We had them left over, and the family looked like they needed some Christmas cheer."

"I doubt they get much in the way of that," he said. "I also noticed how you worried about giving the blanket away. Jacquelyn wouldn't have done that."

"She wouldn't have worried, or she wouldn't have given it away in the first place?"

"Either one."

Mildred, who was stirring the soup, joined the conversation. "I can't believe Jacquelyn would have wanted to stay at the home for this long. I'm surprised she hasn't called by now."

"Maybe she's having fun playing the part of Miss Jane Shaw at the home?" Eddie suggested. "Fooling the girls sounds like something she'd enjoy."

"Maybe." Mildred sounded doubtful.

Eddie turned his attention back to Jane. "What exactly did she say to you about switching clothing?"

Jane cleared her throat. "I want you to understand that this wasn't my idea at all. She insisted."

Eddie nodded. "I believe you. Jacquelyn is known for being impulsive and bending the rules, so this little escapade doesn't surprise me in the least. I am interested in knowing how this happened, though. What did she say exactly?"

Jane set her spoon down and thought back to what Miss Sheridan had said. "She thought it would be funny if we switched clothing and changed our hair so we matched each other. She said I should just keep playing along until you admitted you were wrong, that she and I don't look that much alike."

"Not that much alike!" Mildred exclaimed. "You could be twins." She bustled around the stove, giving the soup one final stir before ladling out a bowl for herself. "The resemblance is remarkable. If I didn't see it with my own two eyes, I wouldn't have believed it."

Eddie grinned and leaned in toward Jane. "My mother should know. She's spent more time with Jacquelyn than anyone else. Jacquelyn has always had a soft spot for my mother."

Oh, so they were mother and son. She could see it now in the light blue eyes and wide smile. Jane thought of something else. "She also said she wanted you to have to eat your words."

"Now that sounds just like her." Eddie chuckled. "Well, I have news for her. I'm not going to admit anything. She'll be the one eating her words."

Mildred joined them at the table. "So you're just going to leave her there, stuck out in the country in a building full of little girls?"

"Not forever," Eddie said. "Maybe for a few more hours? Just until she's forced to surrender. She did tell Jane just to keep playing along, so we're technically following her orders. And you said it yourself, Mother—she hasn't called yet."

"I just hate to think of her being so far from home without the car." Mildred shook her head.

"Jacquelyn Sheridan is resourceful," Eddie said. "And she's never done anything she didn't want to do in her entire life. Believe me, she'll call when she realizes she's overplayed her hand. And who knows, this might change her attitude and she won't be so high and mighty. That would be a Christmas miracle."

"That wouldn't be such a bad outcome," Mildred said slowly. "Maybe this will open her eyes to how other people live. As a child, she was such a sweet little girl. Her heart hardened at some point. I never understood it."

A thought troubled Jane. "But aren't you worried she might get angry and you'll lose your jobs?"

"You are a sweet one, aren't you?" Mildred reached out and patted her arm.

Eddie said, "If Jacquelyn gets mad at anyone it will be me. And I'm not employed here. I can't lose a job I don't have."

"But you drove the car! Aren't you the chauffeur?"

He shook his head. "No, I'm just home for the school break. I attend a university not too far from the girls' home, and when I'm back I like to help out. The Sheridans have been very good to my mother and me. I've lived here since I was a little boy."

"Are you the only ones who work here?"

Mildred laughed. "Heavens, no. There's a whole staff, but all of the others are home for a few days with their families for Christmas."

"Oh, I see," Jane said. But that still didn't address what was going to happen to her. "So we're just going to wait for Miss Sheridan to call?"

Off in the distance, they heard the sound of a door opening and closing. "That would be David, coming home from his appointment," Eddie said.

Was she supposed to know who he was talking about? "David?"

"Jacquelyn's older brother," Mildred said. "He's a dear. Wait until he sees you! He's going to be amazed at the resemblance."

"Hello?" a man's voice called out.

"We're back here." Mildred got up and went to the doorway. "In the kitchen!"

Eddie leaned over the table. "I have an idea. We don't tell David about the switch and see how long it takes him to figure it out."

Mildred turned with one hand on her hip. "He's going to know she's not his sister."

"Maybe not. You said yourself that they could be twins."

Jane said, "I'm not sure I can pull it off." She couldn't even find her way around the mansion yet. Impersonating a close family member was out of the question. Along with that came her own lack of faith in herself. She suspected she wasn't smart enough to pass for a true lady.

"Just try," Eddie said. "Do your best." Seeing the expression on her face he added, "Just for a little while?" He put his hands together as if in prayer.

There was something about Eddie. He had a disarming smile that made her feel as if the two of them were already best friends. It made her want to be part of his secret plan. "All right. I'll try."

"Just follow my lead," he said and winked. "You'll be fine."

Chapter Seventeen

JACQUELYN WOKE UP DISORIENTED. It took a few minutes to realize where she was and to remember all that had transpired. How much time had elapsed since she'd rested her head on this scrunched-up sweater? She wasn't sure.

She climbed out from under the covers and stood, stretching before visiting the lavatory. Afterward, she ventured out into the corridor, looking for Mary. Certainly by now there had to be word from home, saying they were coming back to get her.

But Mary, who was in the kitchen with some older girls preparing a meal, just shook her head. "The telephone hasn't rung, and no one has been here," she said.

"How do you know the phone hasn't rung? You're nowhere near it." Jacquelyn felt indignation rise in her chest.

"I've been having the girls sit in pairs taking turns sitting outside of Mrs. Irving's office," Mary said, chopping a carrot. "They were instructed to come get me the very second that telephone rang. So far, there hasn't been a call."

Jacquelyn begrudgingly gave Mary credit for attending to the telephone. Not that it helped her particular problem. "I've made a decision," she said authoritatively. "I'm going to be leaving soon and going into town, where I'll be hiring a driver to take me home."

Mary lifted her eyes. "That's quite a walk, miss."

"About a mile, isn't that what you said before?"

"About that, give or take. And it's very cold and windy. I'm not sure venturing out today is a good idea."

Jacquelyn scoffed. "The distance won't be a problem for me. I'll just need to eat before I go, and while I'm doing that, I expect you to find a warm coat and boots for me to wear. Oh, and maybe it will be best if you draw a map for me, and I'll need some money as well."

"Some money?" Mary raised her eyebrows. "We could collect every penny in this building and it wouldn't be enough to get you home." Hurriedly she added, "I mean, no disrespect, miss, we just don't have much. And what we do have was hard-earned and not easily replaced."

"I understand. I'll take whatever you can give me. We'll make a note of the amount, and I'll sign it. Then, once I'm safely home, my brother will pay you back in full plus interest. How does that sound?"

"Whatever you wish, Miss Sheridan."

Just what she wanted to hear. "Very good. Let's get started."

Chapter Eighteen

David bounded into the kitchen with a grin on his face, exuding happiness. His very presence lifted the mood in the room. "Ah, just in time for Mildred's famous soup!" he said. "And look at this—Jacquelyn's decided to grace us with her presence! Right here, in the kitchen sitting with the common folk. That's a new one."

Mildred started to get up from the table. "David, why don't you take a seat and relax? I'll get you some soup and bread."

"No, no, no." David motioned for her to sit. "You're eating, Mildred. I can get it." He whistled as he got out a plate, bowl, and silverware, then moved comfortably around the kitchen getting everything he needed. While he was otherwise occupied, Jane felt comfortable watching him. She mentally cataloged the similarities between David and his sister. Their coloring was different, but the shape of the face and nose were the same, which meant he also looked a little bit like her. It was unnerving.

When David got to the table, he directed a question to Jane. "So tell me, how did the visit to the Sheridan Girls' Home go?"

Jane resisted the urge to look at Eddie. "It went fine, thank you. How was your morning?"

David raised his eyebrows. "You're asking about me? That's a new one. Well, if you must know, I had a good meeting with the director of the new Sheridan Food Pantry. We're going to put up notices in local churches and should be able to open in February. Just canned goods at first, but eventually we hope to stock bakery items and fresh produce." As if to illustrate, he held up his piece of bread. "We hope to reach as many people as possible, especially big families and older folks who can't get to the food pantry on the other side of the city. You may not be aware of this, little sister, but there are a lot of hungry people out there. We'll be able to make a big difference."

"That's wonderful!" Jane, who'd planned to say as little as possible, couldn't contain her enthusiasm.

David gave her a sharp look. "These people are really desperate and need help, Jacquelyn. I don't think mocking them is very nice at all."

Jane felt herself shrink back in her chair. "I know. I wasn't mocking them."

Eddie said, "You'll be happy to know that Jacquelyn's visit today has changed everything. She's now open to hearing all of your ideas for the foundation. She wants the foundation to make a difference for the poor."

"Really?"

David's dark eyes were so penetrating she was forced to look down at the table. "Yes," she said.

"Our Jacquelyn is like a completely different person," Eddie continued. "She wants to make the world a better place."

"I hope you're not joking." David's attention was now on Eddie. It was clear he didn't know what to think.

"No joke," Eddie said. "I saw the transformation myself."

"If that's true, how about this?" David's tone was challenging. "We start by buying Christmas gifts for the girls at the home and delivering them tonight?"

"What a lovely idea." Jane clasped her hands together.

"What a lovely idea?" David said, mimicking her. "The last time I brought it up you thought it was ridiculous, that the little urchins already got the gift of free room and board and didn't need anything else."

That was really how Jacquelyn Sheridan talked about them? How appalling. Jane smiled weakly. "I think the girls would love to get Christmas gifts."

"I told you," Eddie said, sitting back triumphantly. "The visit has given her a new view of things. Turns out that behind that beautiful face, there's a girl with a heart after all."

Taking in the compliment, Jane felt her cheeks flush pink. No one had ever called her beautiful.

David spoke to her, jabbing a thumb in Eddie's direction. "You're just sitting there and letting this pass? I can't believe you're not going to give him grief for talking to you that way."

She shook her head.

"No berating him for being disrespectful or not knowing his place?" David looked from her to Eddie and back again, clearly suspicious. "I would love to know what is going through your mind right now."

"You want to know what's going through my mind right now?" Jane asked.

"Yes, I would."

"I was wondering when we could start shopping for the girls' Christmas presents." She was also mulling over what each one would like and hoping she would have some say in the selection. It really didn't matter what they got, though. Even new socks would please the girls. But if it was more than that? Toys or warm mittens or chocolates? Oh, they'd be overjoyed! She could imagine the shouts of glee coming from fifty girls as they each got a Christmas present. The thought filled her with happiness. "If our intent is to drive up and deliver them tonight, we'd really have to start right away."

David looked thoughtful. "You're absolutely right. After lunch, we'll head out. Eddie, I'm assuming you'll want to go along?"

"I wouldn't miss it for anything," he said with a grin. Under the table, he gave Jane's foot a gentle nudge, something that caused a warm flush to wash over her. His smile, aimed right at her, promised secrets and adventure, the likes of which she'd never encountered before.

This was going far better than she'd expected.

Chapter Nineteen

WHEN JACQUELYN HAD SUGGESTED that the girls loan her the money, she hadn't taken into consideration how little they had. Mary had assembled the entire group in the dining area and made an announcement. "Miss Shaw needs to leave now due to a family emergency. I'm asking that anyone who has money contribute it to help her go home. She will make sure you get your money back upon her return."

"A family emergency?" asked a little girl, her brow furrowed in concern. "And at Christmastime too!"

"Oh dear!" another one said. "I do hope no one is sick."

"Someone's probably dead," grumbled an older girl.

"Ruth! That's a terrible thing to say."

"Well, it's true. People get dead all the time."

Mary stepped in to correct the notion. "No one has died, but she does need to leave, and soon. If anyone has money to contribute, go and get it now."

They all took off like a pack of wild animals, leaving their seats and pushing each other aside in an effort to get out the door first. Once they exited, she could hear their footsteps clattering down the hallway.

"Ladies, please!" Mary called after them. "Use your manners." She smiled apologetically at Jacquelyn. "They are excited to be able to contribute. They don't often get a chance to make a difference."

Jacquelyn was strangely touched by their efforts to help her. True, they thought she was Jane, but even so, the emotion was aimed at her. Earlier she'd felt like no one cared, and now she found that wasn't the case.

Twenty minutes later, she had thirty-seven cents in her pocket. Mary had offered up a quarter, while the rest of it was in smaller coins. The littlest girls had offered pennies as if they were gold, opening their clutched fists like they were giving her a present. Even if they'd known she was Miss Sheridan, she wouldn't have the heart to tell them she had more than this in between the cushions of the chair in her bedroom. Seeing her disappointment, Mary whispered, "The girls don't have much, and my salary and Jane's is held for safekeeping by Mrs. Irving."

"For safekeeping?" Jacquelyn frowned. That wasn't right. If it had been her money, she'd insist on having access to it.

"Yes. She says we'll get it when we leave our employment here."

Mary didn't seem a bit bothered by this, but Jacquelyn didn't like the idea. When she got home, she would ask David to look into this Mrs. Irving's accounting practices.

Well, thirty-seven cents was better than nothing. As Mildred was fond of saying, you couldn't get blood from a turnip. After putting on Jane's coat and knit hat and pulling on her winter boots, Jacquelyn went to see how she looked in the mirror in the lavatory. *Appalling* was the word that came to mind. All drab colors and boxy fit. The coat was heavy, like wearing a wool blanket, and it was missing a button halfway down. She imagined getting home and throwing all of it—hat, mittens, coat, boots—straight into the fireplace. She'd let David replace it after it turned to soot. Being able to buy something new for a needy person would bring him such happiness.

Taking the map Mary had drawn for her, she headed out the door and down the long driveway. The winter wind was fierce, making her a tiny bit grateful for the ugly warm coat. Halfway to the road, she stopped to get the mittens from the coat pockets and pulled them on. As she glanced back, she saw a multitude of little faces pressed against the glass, watching her through the windows on the first floor. She raised a hand, and they all waved back. A warm flush came over her at the sight. As a group, they weren't as deplorable as she'd imagined. In fact, that one little girl, Frances, was downright adorable. Jacquelyn felt a bit of admiration for the one they called Ruth as well. That girl actually spoke her mind.

The road had not been well cleared and there weren't any sidewalks, so she had to tread cautiously. No traffic, which shattered the idea that someone might offer to drive her home, or at least into town.

When she rounded a curve and came to a farmhouse, she made an impulsive decision and went up the driveway to the house, knocking on the door.

An older woman with wispy hair and spectacles perched on the end of her nose opened the door. Her brown eyes were so kind that Jacquelyn immediately felt reassured. The old lady said, "Yes? Can I help you, dear?"

"Nellie, who is it?" a man's voice bellowed from the background.

She turned her head and shouted back, "One of the girls from the home!"

Jacquelyn said, "Good afternoon. I'm looking for someone to drive me to Whitefish Bay. I can pay quite well."

Nellie shook her head. "I'm sorry. I can't hear you. You'd best come in." She ushered Jacquelyn inside to the braided rug near the door. Now Jacquelyn could see that this woman had an apron wrapped around her solid middle. The house smelled of baking bread.

"What's all this?" The old man, presumably her husband, came to see what was going on. His overalls and work shirt made Jacquelyn think he was a farmer, not that she knew all that much about country life.

Jacquelyn said, "I need to get home to Whitefish Bay, and I'm looking to hire someone to drive me."

"Whitefish Bay, eh?" he said. "Not sure I know where that is."

"It's near Milwaukee," she said. "About an hour's drive from here?"

"Can you do it?" his wife asked him.

He shook his head. "I don't have the gasoline. How much are you offering?"

"I can pay in full once we arrive. Right now I have thirty-seven cents."

"Thirty-seven cents?" He frowned and gestured to his wife to step to one side. When they were out of earshot, they spoke in whispers, leaving Jacquelyn dripping on the rug.

Getting back to her, the wife said, "I'm sorry, dear, but we won't be able to give you a lift home."

"If it's the money, you don't need to worry about that. I have plenty. Just name your price."

"Oh honey, I'm sure you do have plenty." Was it Jacquelyn's imagination, or did Nellie seem not to believe her? "It's just that we can't take a chance on getting the truck stranded so far from home. I'm sure you understand. But I can give you something to eat for your trip, if you like."

Jacquelyn said, "I do have the money. I'm Jacquelyn Sheridan. My family is one of the wealthiest in the state! I can pay you whatever you want."

The man said, "I'm so sorry. I wish we could help."

"I live in a mansion. I travel to Europe every year. They know me at fashion shows in New York and Paris." So frustrating not to have proof.

"I'm sure they do."

Jacquelyn tried again. "Could I at least use your phone? Just to make a short call?"

"We don't have a phone," he said. "Never saw the need."

They never saw the need? How did they confirm appointments or make travel plans with friends who lived far away? Unbelievable. Well, there was no help to be found here. At least she'd been able to warm up for a few minutes. "Thank you anyway," she said, her hand on the doorknob. "Goodbye, then." Once she was outside, her eyes welled up with tears. Why was life suddenly so hard?

She was nearly to the road when she heard Nellie's voice ring out. "Miss, miss, hold on for a minute."

"Yes?" Jacquelyn turned to see Nellie walking toward her, carrying a cloth bag.

"A sandwich for the road," she said, the bag in her outstretched hand. "God bless you and keep you safe."

"Thank you." The bag was made of a rough fabric with flowers printed on it. A long loop of twine had been sewn onto each side so it could be carried over one shoulder.

"If you want, Arthur can drive you into the village. Someone there might be able to help."

A ride to the village would be most welcome at this point. Jacquelyn gave Nellie a wan smile. "I would like that. Thank you."

Chapter Twenty

J ANE HAD NOT REALIZED how small and contained her life had been until that day. Again, Eddie drove, this time taking his place behind the wheel of a Packard. It was smaller than the Rolls-Royce, but still sleek and elegant. Had she not been impersonating Jacquelyn, she would have stopped to inspect the silver hood ornament depicting a winged boy. Alas, she had to pretend that all of this luxury was something she'd encountered many times before. She feigned indifference and followed Eddie's lead, stepping up on the running board and getting into the back seat while he held the door for her.

Eddie started up the engine. "Downtown Milwaukee, here we come!"

From the front passenger seat, David turned to look at her. "I assume you want to go to Boston Store? That's your favorite."

Before Jane could answer, Eddie chimed in. "We already talked about this and decided Gimbels would have a better selection for gifts."

"That's right," Jane said quietly. She wasn't familiar with either store, but she trusted Eddie's opinion.

Gimbels turned out to be the perfect choice. It had everything the girls had dreamt of, all in one place. She hadn't known a store could be this big or this elegant. Beautifully clad salesgirls stood behind glass cases filled with jewelry and cosmetics, waiting for customers who needed help. The Christmas decorations went beyond anything she could have imagined. Silver Christmas trees had an abundance of shiny ornaments. Twinkling lights were strung along the counters. On every wall was a differently decorated wreath, each one as large as a wagon wheel. In the background, Christmas music played as if the store was filled with hidden radios all set to the same station.

If not for Eddie and David, Jane wouldn't have known what to do. Eddie steered them toward the toy and novelty department. Before they could even begin, a helpful young salesclerk had offered her services. If Jane had been by herself, she would have declined, but David said, "Yes, we do need some help. We'll be buying dozens of gifts that will have to be delivered to Whitefish Bay immediately after we purchase them."

"That won't be a problem at all, Mr. Sheridan," she said.

They know who he is? Jane felt like she was traveling with royalty or movie stars. Surely this was the kind of treatment John Barrymore and Charlie Chaplin received when they were out in public.

David had a list of the girls' names and ages, not that Jane would have needed them, but still it was helpful, since he checked them off as she found gifts for each one. The salesclerk, who introduced herself as Rose, followed in their tracks, taking note of all her choices. Jane felt such joy imagining how each child would feel upon getting her gift. She chose dolls for most of the little girls and toiletry sets for some of the older ones. Each toiletry set came in a leather case and included a comb and brush, items for a manicure, and a hand mirror with an enameled back and handle. All of it was so beautiful she could have cried. "It's not too expensive?" she asked David, who broke into a grin.

"Not at all," he said.

When she saw a toy resembling a Model T, she knew it would be perfect for Ruth, who always commented on automobiles on their walks to school.

"You sure?" David asked.

"Yes," Jane said. "It's just right."

For Dorothy, an aspiring writer, she picked a leather-bound notebook that came with a fancy pen. Oh, she hoped she would be there when Dorothy opened her gift! For Lilian, who had a talent with a sewing needle, she chose a sewing kit. And for Florence, a cross necklace just like the one she talked about her grandma wearing. Jane knew that having it would bring Florence comfort and make her feel closer to her departed grandmother.

Each girl was sure to be delighted with her gift.

Jane's heart expanded with every choice. She didn't think she could be any happier until Eddie said, "What about the two young ladies who work there? I think their names are Jane and Mary?" He cocked his head to one side as if trying to recall.

"Yes," David said, consulting the list. "Jane Shaw and Mary Howard. Both of them grew up in the girls' home and are now employed there, caring for the younger ones."

Jane would have said no to her own gift, but she desperately wanted to get something for Mary. Cautiously, she said, "Do you think that's a good idea?"

"I myself think it's an excellent idea." Eddie gave her that impish grin she found completely endearing.

They wound up at the glove counter in another part of the store. She tried on pair after pair, all of them made with the softest leather. She finally settled on a black pair that had tiny pearl buttons at each wrist. David made sure to tell the clerk they wanted two pairs, one for her and one for Mary.

When they were finished shopping, David took care of the payment and delivery arrangements while she and Eddie waited off to the side. "Will all of the presents fit in the car?" she asked him.

Eddie said, "If not, we can always take two vehicles."

"You would drive two cars so far from home?"

"Of course. Unless you have another idea?" He took a step closer and studied her face.

"No, I think that's fine. It just seems like a lot of trouble and expense for gasoline."

He laughed. "You don't need to worry about that. The Sheridans can well afford it."

What a world the Sheridans lived in! No matter the problem, it could be easily solved. Jane knew money didn't buy happiness, but having access to it sure made life easier.

As they walked out to the car, Eddie said, "What about a stop at the candy shop? We can pick up a few boxes of assorted chocolates as a treat for the girls."

David studied Jane's reaction carefully. "What do you say?"

"I think that's a fine idea." Secretly, she thought it was more than fine. Eddie seemed to instinctively know what would make this the best Christmas ever for a group of girls he didn't even know. After today, she'd probably never see him again, which was a shame, since she was getting awfully fond of having him around.

Chapter Twenty-One

THE INSIDE OF ARTHUR'S truck smelled of manure. The engine was loud and the ride bumpy, not that Jacquelyn was about to complain. As he drove, she thought about what it would have taken to walk the same distance. He'd saved her many steps over a snowy, uneven road, and for that she was grateful. It was hard to believe the girls from the home walked this way and back every school day, but that's what Mary had told her so it must be true. She'd have no reason to tell false tales.

"Here we are!" Arthur said as they approached a cluster of buildings. She'd been warned by Mary that it was a small community and that most of the businesses would be closed because it was a Sunday, but still it was a shock to see that the downtown consisted of so few buildings. Arthur pulled up in front of the church, a modest red brick building with a tall steeple. "You'll want to talk to the pastor. He'll know what to do."

Now that they were there, Jacquelyn felt reluctant to leave the safety of the truck. She pulled Jane's mittens out of her pockets and put them on. "What is the pastor's name?"

"Pastor Mitchell. He's a good man." Snowflakes drifted, lazily landing on the windshield.

"And you think he'll help me?"

"Yes, miss." Arthur's head bobbed an affirmative. "That's what he does."

Part of her wanted to ask Arthur to accompany her inside, but he seemed eager to have her leave the truck. "I hope he's there."

Arthur nodded. "He's probably in his office in the back. If you don't find him there, he and the missus live in the house directly behind the church." He gave her a grandfatherly smile. "Don't worry, miss. You'll be fine."

"Thank you." She looped the cloth bag holding Nellie's sandwich over her shoulder and waited a moment before realizing Arthur wasn't going to come around to her side of the truck and help her down. With a sigh, she opened the door herself, then eased down onto the running board.

"Oh, and miss?" He leaned over.

"Yes?"

"I hope you have a Merry Christmas."

That wasn't likely to happen, not that it was his fault. Switching clothing with Jane Shaw had been a stupid idea. What had she been thinking? Arthur was looking at her expectantly, so Jacquelyn nodded and said, "Thank you."

As he drove away, she felt utterly alone.

Inside, she found the church to be empty, but at least it was warm and inviting, with polished pews and wooden beams overhead. She stamped her feet on the mat and called out, "Hello? Is anyone here?" Her voice echoed off the tall ceiling.

A young woman with a long braid came through an open doorway on the far wall, a mop in her hand. "Can I help you?" Her tone was assured, as if she was used to greeting unexpected visitors.

"Yes, I'm looking for Pastor Mitchell."

"He's not here right now." The young woman's tone was almost cheerful. "Went to hand out Christmas baskets to some of the parishioners. He'll be back before tonight's service, though."

That would be too late. "How about Mrs. Mitchell? I'm told she could help me."

She shook her head. "Both of them went. They do most church functions together."

"Maybe you can help." Jacquelyn strode forward as she talked. "I have a huge problem. I need to hire someone to drive me to Whitefish Bay. It's near Milwaukee. I'm willing to pay quite well. Would you happen to know someone with a car who could benefit from some extra funds this Christmas?"

"No, sorry."

No, sorry? That couldn't be right. There was a *depression* on. All everyone talked about was money, money, money and how there weren't enough jobs for the working-class folks. It was in the newspaper every single day. Even at parties, conversations drifted into the state of the economy. At times it seemed as if the topic was all people could talk about. Sometimes Jacquelyn was so sick of it she felt like screaming. And now this woman—*girl, really*—was summarily dismissing her proposition out of hand without even pausing to consider it?

"I'm not sure you understand. I have money. Lots of money. I'm willing to pay and pay well for someone to chauffeur me to my home in Whitefish Bay. I'm Jacquelyn Sheridan. Surely you've heard of me and my family?"

The young woman leaned against her mop. "I'm sorry for your troubles, miss, but folks around here don't have much. Not too many people have reliable cars for a long trip like that. And if they do, they don't have the gasoline to get 'em there." She shrugged. "Today's not the best time either. Most people have plans the day before Christmas."

"I understand that," Jacquelyn said impatiently, "but surely *someone* can help? As I said before, I'm willing to pay."

The girl raised her eyebrows. "You have the cash with you?"

"Well, no, but I can pay once we arrive at my home in Whitefish Bay. It's a mansion with a view of the lake."

"Not being able to pay up front is a problem." She gave Jacquelyn a sympathetic look. "But if you want to stay here and warm up for a while, miss, you're more than welcome. Pastor always says never to turn anyone away. He believes in being generous to the poor."

"I'm not poor," Jacquelyn said, but her protests appeared to fall on deaf ears as the girl had begun to mop. "I'm only dressed like this because I switched clothing with someone at the girls' home. As a lark. I thought it would be funny. Now she's wearing my fine dress and I'm stuck in this rag." Earlier, the idea of the switch had struck her as being hilarious, but now she felt like crying. The hole she'd dug for herself was getting deeper by the hour. In the meantime, where were Eddie and Jane? She had a sudden thought that the Rolls-Royce had broken down or they'd been in some sort of collision. If that were the case, she could be stuck here for a long time.

The young woman flipped her braid over one shoulder and kept mopping. "The girls' home. I thought you looked familiar. You're Jane, aren't you? One of the older ones who works there?"

"No, I'm not Jane, but there's a resemblance. People say we look alike," Jacquelyn said miserably, wishing she looked like anyone else in the world. She toed the floor, tracing around a swirl in the wood grain. "That's why I thought it would be funny to wear each other's clothing. To see who would notice."

"If you're really from that rich family, why don't you call them and have someone come and collect you?"

Jacquelyn lifted her head. "Do you have a telephone?"

"Yes, indeed. Pastor has one at home. He doesn't normally let folks use it, though." She gripped the mop handle. "And you're talking about calling long distance. That can get expensive."

Jacquelyn said, "I have thirty-seven cents that I'll gladly hand over if I can use the telephone."

The woman pursed her lips, considering. "That should more than cover it. At least if you don't talk long."

"Oh, thank you!" Progress at last. "I won't talk long at all."

She leaned the mop against the wall. "Follow me."

Chapter Twenty-Two

THE AROMA OF CHOCOLATE in the candy store was heavenly. Best yet, when David announced their intent to purchase two of their largest boxes of assorted chocolates, the bald man behind the counter, the owner, gave them samples to eat right on the spot. Jane couldn't believe that he'd just handed over candy for free, but David and Eddie were blasé about this unexpected offer of generosity, taking the delicately swirled pieces of chocolate and popping them into their mouths as if this were no big deal. The chocolate she'd been given was something called a truffle. Jane decided it was the most delicious thing she'd ever eaten in her entire life.

Overwhelmed by all the choices, she let David choose which chocolates should be included in the assortment. As the men talked, she found herself oddly mesmerized by an older lady behind the counter using a pastry bag to fill what seemed to be a mold. *Oh, so that's how they do it!*

The owner handed her another sample, this time a candy bar in a foil wrapper, and said, "A beautiful gift for the beautiful lady." She gratefully accepted it, but she didn't open the foil wrapper. If only she had a way to share it with Mary! But of course, Mary would be getting a taste of the chocolate they were currently buying. She and the other girls were going to love the treats.

After all of the candy was chosen, the boxes were wrapped in brown paper and tucked into a paper bag for the trip home. Eddie took charge of the bag, while David held the door. Eddie offered his arm as insurance against the icy sidewalk, something that Jane gratefully accepted. A flutter came over her when he glanced down at her and smiled mischievously. David, who walked ahead of them, didn't notice.

They were nearly to where they'd parked when a little boy of about seven or eight approached them. "I'll carry your bag for a nickel, mister," he said, with a hopeful smile. "I'm very strong."

"No, thank you," Eddie said with a nod. "It's actually not heavy at all."

David added, "We don't need any assistance, thanks."

"Wait a minute." Jane stopped in her tracks and addressed the child. "What would you do with a nickel if you got one?"

"Give it to my mother, of course," he said earnestly. "We could buy a loaf of bread with that much." He had a dirt smudge on one cheek. Jane had to hold back the urge to wipe it clean.

She turned to David. "Don't you have a nickel to give?"

David gave her a curious look but stuck his hand in his pocket and pulled out a quarter. "I'll give this to you as long as you promise not to announce it to the world. Just take it quietly and go straight home to your mother."

"Yes, sir! I promise."

"Give this to your mother too," Jane said, handing him the candy bar.

The little boy's face lit up in amazement. "Oh boy! Thank you, miss."

"Remember, not a word." David held out the coin.

"Not a word." He crossed his heart before snatching the coin out of David's hand. "Thank you, mister." The boy was true to his promise, running quickly in the opposite direction.

On the ride home, Jane asked David, "Why did you tell that boy not to say a word after you gave him the money?"

Eddie answered on his behalf. "Because he didn't want us to suddenly be surrounded by a pack of children begging for money."

David said, "That's exactly it. If you give to one, the next thing you know there's more. It's heartbreaking running out of money and having to look in their eyes and tell them no. They're just children, and they're out in the cold begging. But of course, you wouldn't know anything about that, Jacquelyn. You so rarely leave your crystal palace." His tone was dry, but the words were biting. Clearly, there was animosity between the brother and sister.

The truck from Gimbels arrived shortly after their own arrival at the mansion. Jane and Eddie went inside, while David directed the delivery on the driveway. Even though Jane had been at the Sheridans' earlier, the feeling of awe upon seeing the grandeur of the home was just as strong. It wasn't a crystal palace, but it came close.

Standing in the front hall, Eddie said to Jane, "David clearly knows something is up. Your generosity has made him very suspicious. I think we should tell him."

Jane let out a sigh of relief. "I'm so glad to hear you say this. I've been feeling guilty."

"I think it's gone on long enough. We'll tell him, and then we'll drive the gifts up and you and Jacquelyn can switch back. No harm done."

"Why do you think Miss Sheridan hasn't called already?"

Eddie shrugged. "It's hard to say. My guess is that she's having too much fun deceiving innocent children. I may be wrong, though."

"You don't seem that worried about her."

"If it were anyone else, I'd worry. Jacquelyn is another story. She has a commanding presence. She always gets what she wants. Believe me, if she wanted to be here, she'd be here. Chances are, she's dead set on making her point and isn't about to give in."

Jane remembered Jacquelyn's commanding presence because she'd fallen prey to it herself. Somehow, against her better judgment, Jane had been convinced to switch clothes and assume another identity. The power behind that couldn't be denied.

David came in then, followed by two men in brown uniforms who went back and forth carrying boxes from the store. He directed them into the dining room, where they set everything on the table.

A radio on top of a sideboard had been left on and was playing a dramatic story. Eddie spun the dial until he found a station playing Christmas music. "Now we're in business!" he said, flashing a smile.

Something was happening between them, but Jane couldn't put her finger on exactly what it was. A feeling of familiarity combined with a soft pang of yearning? Maybe. She was so inexperienced in the ways of the world, but this felt a little like the beginnings of love. Of course, that was ridiculous. She barely knew him.

In the midst of this commotion, Mildred came out, wiping her hands on her apron. "I've just finished baking cookies to take to the rescue mission for their holiday celebration. That, along with all these lovely presents, finally makes it feel like Christmas." She grinned. "I'll go and get the wrapping paper and string."

Jane had never heard of wrapping Christmas gifts. She'd gotten presents as a child when her mother was alive, but they were always under the tree when she got up in the morning. No wrapping, just the gifts. Now, she played along and did what the others were doing, covering each package with decorative paper and tying them with string. With four of them, they were able to make fast work of it.

Every now and then she caught David giving her a puzzled look from across the table. Was she supposed to be the one telling him the truth? Somehow it felt like it was Eddie's responsibility, but she couldn't manage to get his attention.

Jane was tasked with writing each girl's name on her particular gift. "Some people like to use sealing wax to hold the paper in place,"

Mildred said, "but I've always found that to be messy. I guess I'm just old-fashioned."

"I think they look perfect with the string," Jane said. She looked to Eddie. "Weren't we going to tell David something?" Her time here had been eye-opening and lovely in so many ways, but she was more than ready to cast off her role as Jacquelyn and just be Jane again.

David, who'd been concentrating on cutting a piece of paper, said, "What's that?"

She blurted it out. "I'm not who you think I am. I'm Jane Shaw from the Sheridan Girls' Home. Your sister had me switch clothing with her to see if anyone would notice the difference."

"You're not Jacquelyn?" He narrowed his eyes.

"No, I'm not. I'm sorry to deceive you. I wanted to say something, but your sister was very clear on keeping it to myself until someone figured it out." She gestured to Eddie. "And then Eddie thought—"

David interrupted, talking to Eddie. "You knew about this the whole time?"

"Yes." Eddie looked a little sheepish. "I'd told Jacquelyn there was a young woman who worked at the home who could be her double. Apparently, she was trying to prove that there wasn't a strong resemblance, but since you, her own brother, didn't see it, I think that backs my case."

"They do look identical," Mildred said. "If I hadn't been there the day Jacquelyn was born, I'd have thought they were twins."

"You *knew* too?" David's tone was incredulous.

"Yes," Mildred said. "Since lunchtime. We were certain you'd see it right away."

David pushed his chair away from the table and came around to get a closer look at Jane. He motioned for her to stand and then leaned in to stare, making her very uncomfortable. He walked from side to side, studying every angle of her face. When he was done, he stepped back and shook his head. "Remarkable."

"I'm so sorry," she said. Somehow this bit of trickery no longer felt like the innocent fun Jacquelyn had proposed. She found herself holding her breath, waiting for the consequences. Certainly he would be mad, and she couldn't blame him.

Finally, he said, "It's uncanny. I mean, I can see the difference, but only because I'm looking for it."

"Isn't it something?" Eddie said. "Jane has her own personality, but on the outside, they're a match."

David threw his head back and laughed. "I hope you made a bet with my sister. I'd love to see you win some money over this."

"No bet," Eddie said. "In fact, she did it without telling me. She thought I'd immediately see the difference, proving her point, but it didn't work out that way."

"Is she waiting in the wings?" he asked, glancing at the doorway. "Jacquelyn, you can come out now!"

"She's not here," Eddie said. "She's still at the girls' home. She was playing the part of Jane when it was time to go, and no one noticed the difference. I actually thought I had Jacquelyn in the back seat when I drove away. It wasn't until we were nearly home that I figured it out."

Sheepishly, Jane added, "She told me not to say anything. I'm so sorry."

"So you left her there?" David was clearly having trouble understanding the way the day's events had unfolded.

"Not on purpose," Eddie said quietly.

Jane added, "I'm so sorry. I wanted to say something."

"I can't believe you left her there." David shook his head. "She has to be miserable. We have to go get her."

Eddie said, "That's our plan. When we drive up to deliver the gifts, the girls can switch back." He directed his attention to Jane. "But I, for one, will be sad to see Miss Shaw go. I've been enjoying her company all day."

Mildred held up one finger. "Shush, I think I hear the phone ringing."

They all cocked their heads, listening over the sound of "Jingle Bells" on the radio. "That *is* the phone," David said, heading out the door. "I'll get it."

Chapter Twenty-Three

As it turned out, the young woman with the mop was Pastor Mitchell's daughter, Pauline. She led Jacquelyn across the courtyard to the unassuming white clapboard cottage behind the church. In the back of the house was Pastor Mitchell's office. Jacquelyn set the thirty-seven cents next to the telephone on his desk and picked up the receiver. It took some explaining for the operator to understand the logistics of the long-distance call, but finally, after the operator spoke with the switchboard in Milwaukee, the connection was made.

Jacquelyn ran her finger over the cloth-covered cord, waiting anxiously. What she wouldn't give to hear Mildred's voice on the other end of the line! Darling Mildred, who would certainly sympathize with the suffering she'd endured that day. As soon as she walked in the door at home, she'd request a warm bath and a hot meal.

Still listening, she gripped the cord as if it were a lifeline, feeling Pauline's eyes boring into her. She wished she would go away. When the operator came back, she said, "I'm sorry, Miss Sheridan, but no one is answering. Please try again later."

"Wait! Wait!" she cried out, but the sound of the click coming through the receiver indicated it was too late.

"No one is home?" Pauline asked, her tone sympathetic.

"No," Jacquelyn said. "So odd. Mildred never leaves. She's very dependable." She'd never given it much thought until that very moment. Mildred had always just been there for her. As constant as the rising sun. And now, it appeared, she was gone.

Fear gripped her heart and made her question why this would be. What if Eddie had crashed the automobile and now he and Jane were in the hospital? That would explain why neither David nor Mildred was home to answer the phone. Both of them would rush to the hospital if they knew Jacquelyn and Eddie were injured. David had always given her trouble, but his steadfastness, his reliability, was something she valued. Now, she felt as if her grip on the edge of a cliff had come loose and she was tumbling into oblivion.

Her whole world had unraveled.

"So what are you going to do?" Up close, with her wide eyes, Pauline looked much younger. Fourteen at the most.

Jacquelyn mulled it over. The Sheridan money had to count for something in this village. She was going to find someone to help her if it was the last thing she did. She scooped up the thirty-seven cents.

"I can tell you one thing—I'm going to be home for Christmas, no matter what it takes."

Chapter Twenty-Four

When David returned to the dining room fifteen minutes later, he had a troubled look on his face.

"Who was it?" Mildred asked.

"I got there too late to answer," he said. "Just as I put my hand on the receiver, it stopped ringing."

"Couldn't have been Jacquelyn, then." Mildred pursed her lips and shook her head. "She wouldn't have given up so easily."

David didn't look convinced. "I wouldn't be so sure of that. I just called the Sheridan Girls' Home. It took some time, but I finally got through and talked to Mary Howard. It seems that my sister left a little over an hour ago."

"So she's on her way here?" Jane hoped that was the case.

David said, "Not necessarily. She left to walk into town to find someone to drive her home. Mary said that she only had thirty-seven cents on her. Apparently, they took up a collection for her and that's all they could come up with."

Jane was surprised they'd come up with that much. The girls rarely had money, and if Mrs. Irving got wind of it, she held on to the cash for safekeeping.

David continued. "Mary said it's quite cold and windy there and that she found it unlikely that Jacquelyn would find someone to drive her all the way to Whitefish Bay, especially the day before Christmas. Even after warning her of all this, my sister would not be dissuaded."

In the background, the radio played the song "Joy to the World," the uplifting words a contrast to the conversation in the room.

Mildred set down her scissors. "But why didn't Jacquelyn call if she wanted to come home? You boys could have been up there in no time."

"The topic of calling home did come up," David said. "Apparently, the director of the home has a lock on the telephone to prohibit unauthorized calls. Jacquelyn wanted to call but couldn't remove the lock to dial the operator."

"She must have been furious," Eddie said, suddenly serious.

"Yes, and when she's angry she doesn't always make the best decisions," David said, folding his arms. "Frankly, I'm worried."

His worry caused Jane's breath to catch in her chest. If Jacquelyn Sheridan, the heiress of the Sheridan family, was injured or killed and her actions had played a part in causing it, she would never forgive herself. She should have just said no. That's all there was to it. She'd been spineless. If only she'd listened to her intuition and refused to change clothing, none of this would have happened.

If only.

The truth was, though, that secretly she'd always *wanted* a taste of a different life. A better life. But was it better? More comfortable, certainly, but it didn't feel like a good fit for her, probably because it wasn't rightfully hers. And now Miss Sheridan was out in the cold, alone and lost, and Jane was to blame.

"So what do you think we should do?" Mildred asked. "Call the police?"

David shook his head. "No, not just yet. She was fine an hour ago. I think Miss Shaw and I need to drive up to the girls' home. You and Eddie stay here and keep on top of the telephone. With any luck, she's gotten discouraged and walked back to the home, but if that's not the case, she'll find a telephone somewhere and try calling again." He exhaled. "My sister is nothing if not persistent when she wants something."

"How will we know what happens with you once you leave?" Mildred asked. "Not knowing is going to make me a nervous wreck."

"I'll call you when we arrive and let you know what we find out," David said. "Someone in the village has to have seen her. She couldn't have gone far."

Eddie stood up. "I'd be happy to go with you to take Miss Shaw home. It won't take two people to guard the telephone." He gave Jane an encouraging look.

"Nice try," David said, "but you're staying here. I'm fully capable of driving, and it's my sister who's missing. Besides, your mother will need you to drop off the cookies at the mission. We don't have room for you in the Rolls anyway. We need the space for the presents." He gestured to the mound on the other end of the table. "But since you're so set on being of service, you can help me carry these out." His gaze went from Eddie to Jane and back again, as if to show he knew Eddie's real interest was not in the well-being of Jacquelyn Sheridan.

"Of course," Eddie said, meeting David's eyes. "You know I'm always glad to help."

Chapter Twenty-Five

THE EDGE OF DOWNTOWN Newtonville started with the church and grammar school and stretched on in one straight line. And that line wasn't very long. This village fit the very definition of a one-horse town, not that Jacquelyn saw any horses. Luckily, a sidewalk lined the front of the buildings, so she had a safe place to walk.

As Mary had warned, most of the businesses were closed. The bakery, the post office, and the butcher shop all had hand-printed signs hanging on the inside of the doorways that indicated they were closed for the holidays but would be open on December 26. As if that would help her.

She pressed her face against the glass window of a fabric shop that still had lights on, but she didn't see anyone inside. She knocked for good measure, but there was no response. Christmas wasn't until tomorrow. Why wasn't anyone working? Hadn't they heard of last-minute shopping? In the city, the department stores would be filled with throngs of shoppers right now. She herself often shopped the day of Christmas Eve, taking in the stores' festive decorations and the lines of children waiting to see Santa.

A truck drove toward her and she raised her arm for them to stop, but the old man inside mistook her gesture for a wave and returned the greeting as he went past. She sighed and continued on.

Store after store disappointed her, all the way to the end of the shopping district. Farther down, she saw signs of life surrounding a building off in the distance. Vehicles lined the street in front of it, and as she watched, the door was flung open and a man stumbled out. The distant sound of music followed him out, only lasting until the door slammed shut. A smile stretched across her face. *Finally!* Evidence of life in this burg. As the man wandered off, Jacquelyn quickened her steps.

Getting closer, she saw the sign. *The Mule.* Twenty yards beyond, the stumbling man leaned over and vomited into the street. From that and the beer sign in the window, she surmised that she'd found the village tavern. Well, while it certainly wasn't a place she'd usually visit, the fact of the matter was that liquor and men went together, and judging by the trucks and automobiles in front, they had transportation. Maybe one of them would like to make some quick and easy money the day before Christmas.

Inside, the air was warm and damp, an improvement from being out in the cold. A half dozen men were seated at the bar, and a handful more were sitting at two tables. A haze of cigarette smoke hung in the air. Behind the bar, a large older woman poured whiskey into a line of shot glasses. When done, she raised her eyes and noticed Jacquelyn with surprise. "What have we here?" she said, her voice husky.

Jacquelyn strode authoritatively to the end of the bar and spoke loudly enough for all to hear. "I'm looking to hire someone to drive me to Whitefish Bay." Seeing their blank stares, she added, "It's near Milwaukee. I can pay well."

"How much you willing to pay?" one grizzled old man asked.

"How much are you proposing?" The Sheridans might have bank accounts bulging at the seams, but that didn't mean she was going to just throw money to the wind. Her father always said that a hard bargain could be easily won, if a person was thoughtful and prudent.

"Fifty dollars!" He stood up and banged a fist on the bar. "And not a penny less."

Every man in the place burst into uproarious laughter. Somehow she'd wandered into the sole Newtonville tavern and found a group of men who thought her misery was funny.

"All right, then," she said, turning to address the crowd. "I'll pay fifty dollars to the first man who is willing to leave and drive me home right now."

The woman behind the bar cackled. "They must pay better at the home than I thought."

"For fifty dollars, I'll do it," came a shout from the back.

"No, I'll do it," said one of the men drinking beer at the closest table.

"What the hell, I'll do it!"

"Let me take you, miss."

The old man who'd pounded on the bar said, "Show me the money and we can leave right now."

"I don't have the money with me at the moment." As soon as the words were out, all of their enthusiasm disappeared.

"Knew it was too good to be true."

"April Fools' came early, I guess."

"No! I'm completely serious!" she cried out. "I swear to you that my family is very wealthy. I'm only dressed like this because I was pulling a prank. I'm Jacquelyn Sheridan. I'm sure you've heard the name."

"I know the name, but you ain't one of them." This came from a dark corner in the back of the room.

"Wealthy my foot. She looks about as poor as a church mouse."

She fished around in her pocket and pulled out her change. "I have thirty-seven cents, which I can pay up front as a goodwill gesture. The balance will be paid upon my return home."

"How do we know you'll pay it once you get there?"

"I give you my word," she said solemnly.

"Eh." One of the men at the bar slapped his hand in the air as if waving away a pesky fly. "You're going to have to do better than that."

Those on the barstools turned away from her, clearly having lost interest.

"I'll swear on the Bible, if need be!" she cried out. "I'm worried about my family, and I need to get home."

Her words did not persuade them. They began talking to each other, making a point to ignore her. Couldn't they see she needed help? They were only judging her by the flimsiest of evidence, the clothes on her back. How could they be so hateful, especially so close to Christmas?

The lady behind the bar looked up from wiping the counter. "Maybe you have something in that bag you could use for barter?" She gestured to the cloth bag draped over her shoulder, the one that held Nellie's sandwich.

"No, I don't have anything of value."

"Are you interested in a drink, then, miss?"

"No, thank you," Jacquelyn said, blinking back tears.

"Then you'd best be moving on." She pointed to the door with a jab of her thumb. "There's nothing for you here."

Chapter Twenty-Six

David and Eddie were able to get all the presents in the trunk and back seat of the Rolls-Royce. As David was holding the front passenger door open for Jane, Eddie, who'd disappeared a few moments earlier, came running out with a blanket draped over his arm. "Don't forget this!" he said, holding a plaid blanket similar to the one she'd given away.

"So you did have another one of those!" she said, giving him a smile.

"I told you—we have a dozen or so. I think they multiply in the closet on their own. Feel free to bestow this one on another cold child if need be. We won't suffer from its absence." Jane's hand rested on the window frame, and Eddie's fingers brushed against it as he handed her the blanket, giving her a thrill. "You take care of yourself, Jane. I hope we meet again."

"I hope so as well."

He was still looking at her as David started up the automobile and pulled away from the house. She glanced backward as they went down the driveway, and he was still standing there, his hand raised in a goodbye.

When the automobile turned onto the road, David said, "I think Eddie is going to miss you. Funny, you look just like my sister and the two of them never got along, but he seems quite taken with you."

Jane wasn't quite sure what to say. She'd found playacting as Jacquelyn to be awkward and fraught with emotion, so much so that she and Eddie hadn't really gotten a chance to talk and get acquainted. She'd only just met him that day, but oddly enough, she was now sure she would miss him. Finally, she said, "He seems like a fine young man."

"He is. One of the best. And I can tell he really likes you."

And I can tell he really likes you. She wanted to take those words and put them in her pocket and take them out on gray days when she needed a bit of cheer. Would anyone ever look at her like that again? It was hard to imagine.

Riding in the front seat of the Rolls-Royce was a different experience than being a passenger in the back. The dashboard was polished wood with dials that reminded her of clocks. One was labeled "Oil," and another seemed to indicate how fast they were going. Others were a mystery. She didn't have a lot of experience being in automobiles and was fascinated by the mechanics of it, the pedals on the floor and the way David strong-armed the steering wheel in order to turn a corner. She had the sense that she should be taking in everything while she could. Very soon, her life would be back to her old routine. She'd be braiding hair and doing laundry and tucking little girls into bed. All admirable tasks and certainly necessary, but now that she knew how big the world was, it all seemed a bit small.

David said, "A penny for your thoughts."

She smiled. "I'm not sure my thoughts are worth a penny." They'd left the wealthy area of the Sheridans' neighborhood and were heading toward the city. She remembered doing this ride in reverse earlier. Had it really been the same day? So much had changed in so little time.

"I'm sure whatever you're thinking about is worth much more than a penny. Tell me about your life. How did you come to work at the home?"

He seemed sincerely interested, so before she knew it, she was recounting her whole life story—her missing father and the death of her mother, how her aunt had sent her to Newtonville, promising she'd have fun with the other girls. From the way David kept asking questions, one would have thought she was the most fascinating person in the world. "You were six years old and they put you on a bus all by yourself?"

"Well, I wasn't completely by myself. There were other people on the bus."

"I know, but . . ." They were at a stop sign, and he turned to look her way. "You were so little. That must have been very frightening." His eyes filled with sympathy.

"It was." She remembered climbing the steps to the bus. The driver had extended a hand and helped her up the stairs, then took charge of her suitcase. She'd wanted to turn and run, but there was nowhere to go. "I was afraid."

"You're very brave, Jane Shaw," he said solemnly.

"I didn't have a choice." No one had asked her what she wanted. She'd been a child. Life had just been inflicted upon her. "It was hard, but things got better eventually."

By the time they saw a sign saying, "Newtonville, 2 miles," Jane had recounted the details of her entire life, including that morning. She ended by saying, "And now I have a question for you, Mr. Sheridan."

"Please, call me David. And feel free to ask any question you'd like."

"How is it that you plan to call Eddie and Mildred once we arrive at the home? If Mary and Jacquelyn couldn't make a call because the telephone was locked, it stands to reason you'll have the same trouble."

David grinned. "I'm not worried about that. They used to secure the phones in the university offices in the same way, and a friend and I figured out a way to jimmy the locks."

"Really? There's a way to do that?"

"There's a way to do almost everything if you want it badly enough."

Jane wanted to believe he was right, although personally she hadn't found that to be the case in her own life. Maybe in his world that's how it worked.

David slowed as they approached the downtown area. "If you don't mind, I'd like to make a few stops and see if anyone has seen my sister."

"Of course. What a good idea."

He steered to the side of the road and shut off the engine in front of the Mule. "I'll only be a minute. If you don't mind waiting? It doesn't look like the sort of place a lady should be entering."

No one had ever called her a lady before. She suppressed a grin at the notion. "I don't mind at all. Take your time. I'll be fine."

While he was inside, Jane arranged the blanket over her lap, thinking of how Eddie had remembered that she might get cold while traveling. So thoughtful of him. The interior windows were beginning to ice up by the time David returned. He slid into his seat and said, "It seems Jacquelyn was here more than an hour ago, trying to hire someone to drive her home."

"No one would do it?"

He shook his head. "She didn't have much money on her, and no one believed she was rich. They laughed at her, is what I was told. My poor sister must be nearly hysterical by now. Jacquelyn can be bossy and loud, so she seems strong, but believe me, she's not nearly as capable or brave as you are. She's used to having things come easily."

Wearing Jane's clothes hadn't done Jacquelyn any favors. Jane felt a pang of guilt. "Oh, I'm sorry to hear that. Maybe she returned to the home, then?"

"Maybe," David said. "One of them suggested trying the church. Everything else is closed right now." He held his palm to the foggy window to clear a spot.

Jane followed suit, doing the same on her side. Now there were two circles of visibility on the windshield. "Pastor Mitchell would have helped her, I just know it. He's a very kind man."

"I hope she's there," David said. "If not, she might have returned and is now with Mary and the girls. She couldn't have gone far."

Chapter Twenty-Seven

JACQUELYN WAS NOT GOING to admit defeat that easily. Standing outside the Mule, she weighed her options. She could return to the Sheridan Girls' Home and admit Mary was right, or keep going and see if anyone else in this sad little village was willing to help her.

She walked to the edge of the building and turned down a side street. At the first house, she knocked and peered in the window, but no one answered. After a few moments, she gave up and continued on to the next house, thinking it couldn't be worse.

As it turned out, it was worse. Since the front walkway hadn't been shoveled, she was forced to trudge through snowdrifts to the dilapidated front porch. Getting closer, she noticed one of the windows was boarded up. She rapped on the door anyway, even though it quickly became clear no one had lived there in a long time. Why didn't they tear the house down if it was such a wreck? So much of how people lived puzzled her.

She gave up and kept going.

At the end of the block, a narrow road ran parallel to the railroad tracks. Jacquelyn guessed that following it would take her back to the girls' home. Not her desired destination, but sadly, if she didn't find a driver soon, it might come to that. She wasn't about to freeze to death wearing Jane Shaw's dreadful coat and boots, not to mention the drab dress underneath.

She walked down the narrow road, which was thankfully clear of snow. When the tracks curved, so did the road. Following it, she got a whiff of campfire smoke and then saw the source off in the distance. A man stood near a rusty barrel, warming himself over flames flickering out of the top. "Hello, miss," he said, giving her a friendly wave.

A hobo.

She'd often heard about hobos but had never seen one. This man fit the description, down to his disheveled appearance and the knapsack at his feet. He was welcoming, though, which was more than she'd encountered at the Mule. "Hello," she responded.

"Get closer and warm up," he said, beckoning to the fire. "Come on. I don't bite."

She considered the invitation, but it only took a second to decide she was cold and stopping for a moment couldn't hurt. Joining him near the barrel, she held her mitten-clad hands a safe distance from the fire. "Why does it have to be so cold?" she wondered aloud.

He laughed. "I ask myself that quite a lot, actually. Except in summertime, when I complain that it's too hot." He smiled. It was a pleasant smile, even with the one missing tooth on the bottom. "Name's Ezra, by the way."

"Jacquelyn Sheridan. It's a pleasure to meet you."

If the Sheridan name meant anything to him, it didn't show. "It's real nice to meet you, young lady. And where might you be off to, on such a cold winter's day right before Christmas?"

"I desperately need to get home." She took off a mitten to wipe the tears from her eyes. "I've tried everything, but no one will help me." Her voice was choked with emotion.

"That's a shame," he said, sympathy crossing his whiskered face. "Where is home?"

She sniffed. "Whitefish Bay. It's near Milwaukee."

"Why, I'm leaving for Milwaukee soon!" He fished out a pocket watch and flipped open the cover. "The train will be heading out in less than an hour. You can come along with me, if you like."

"There's a train that goes to Milwaukee?" Why had no one mentioned this?

"Yes, ma'am." Ezra's head bobbed an affirmative. "Stops at the switching yard down a ways and goes from there."

"How much is a ticket? I only have thirty-seven cents." She had no idea how much things cost. During shopping trips she'd have her purchases put on the family's account, and the bookkeeper settled up when the invoices arrived. When traveling, that same bookkeeper arranged for all of her expenses. Before today, she'd considered carrying money to be common and dirty. Who knew how many people had handled the paper and coins? Now she'd give anything to have a wad of it in her pocket.

"I have a friend who gets me on for a quarter," Ezra said. "I can get the same deal for you."

"Really?" It sounded too good to be true, but it was worth a try. "I'd be so grateful if you would. I need to get home." Now the tears were starting again.

"Of course. That's what everyone wants at Christmastime." He tilted his head. "You poor thing. I'm sorry for your troubles."

At that moment, it seemed like Ezra was the only person in the world who understood her pain. "Yes, I'd love to take you up on your kind offer. Thank you."

"You're welcome. It will be nice to have the company."

Jacquelyn had often heard that hobos would rob you blind given the chance, but she considered herself a good judge of character and this man seemed harmless. "I have had a terrible day." The words came out, and as he nodded encouragingly, she kept going, spilling all the details of her time in Newtonville. She'd just finished talking when they heard a train horn farther down the tracks. Turning toward the noise, she saw the black locomotive coming to a stop alongside a platform with a roof over it. A truck was parked nearby.

"She's here!" Ezra said, taking out his pocket watch again. "And right on time too."

Such a relief. Soon she'd be home.

"Come along, and move quickly." He gestured for her to follow him. "Stick with me and let me do the talking."

"Can we just leave the fire?" she asked, glancing backward as they walked away.

"It's not going anywhere." He shrugged. "It'll put itself out."

When they got closer to the train, he crossed the tracks to the other side and led her to the cars in the back. A younger man wearing a cap with ear flaps waved them over, a cross look on his face. "Hurry up," he hissed. "My boss is here today."

Ezra quickened his steps, and Jacquelyn followed suit. "I got my quarter ready," he said, holding it out. "She's coming with me."

"She better be paying too. I'm not running a charity."

"I have the money," Jacquelyn said, offended. She fumbled with taking off her mittens, then reached into her pocket and pulled out Mary's quarter.

"Took ya long enough," the man grouched, plucking it out of her palm. He turned to the train door and yanked it open. "Get in quick."

Jacquelyn took a step back. This was not the passenger train she'd been envisioning.

Ezra scrambled up into the train car, then extended a hand for Jacquelyn. For a split second, she considered staying behind, but she'd already paid and was out of options. She grabbed his hand and allowed him to pull her aboard. As soon as she was inside, the man who'd taken her money slid the door shut.

It closed with a firm and resounding clank.

Chapter Twenty-Eight

DAVID AND JANE STOPPED at the church, where they discovered that Jacquelyn had visited earlier and spoken to Pastor Mitchell's daughter. "At least we know that she was the one who made the phone call. It's too bad I didn't answer in time," David said as they returned to the automobile. After that, they drove to the home. David went to the front door and spoke to Mary while Jane waited.

"My sister hasn't been back," he said upon returning to the Rolls-Royce. "I'm very worried. Where could she be? Anyone else could manage, but she doesn't know anything about the ways of the world." His face creased with concern. "And it's so cold out."

"Is there anything I can do to help?" Jane asked.

"Just pray."

She nodded and bowed her head, praying silently. Out of the corner of her eye, she noticed David doing the same.

When they finished, he said, "Maybe Mildred will have heard from her. In the meantime, let's just follow your plan."

David drove to the back door of the building, where they unloaded presents into the storage room to hide them until Christmas morning. Mary had made sure the girls were nowhere around.

David said, "Mary thought it best to give the girls the gifts after you return from church tomorrow morning. She said if you gave the presents to them beforehand, they'd be too excited to sit still during the service."

"She's absolutely right." As eager as Jane was to see them open their gifts, she knew that getting overly excited often caused some of the girls to misbehave. Making mischief in church would not have reflected well on the Sheridan Girls' Home.

Mary popped her head in the door. "I brought a change of clothes so you can return home as yourself."

"Good idea," Jane said, taking the pile of clothes out of her hands. Mary nodded and left just as quickly as she'd arrived.

Once the Rolls-Royce was emptied and all of the gifts piled near the canned goods, David went to wait in the automobile while she changed clothing. When she came out, she carried the dress, shoes, and coat folded in a pile, which she put in the back seat. "You could keep Jacquelyn's things, you know," David said. "She has so much, she probably won't miss them."

Jane shook her head. "I would never do that. They don't belong to me."

David started up the engine and drove around to the front of the building. Mary had left the front door unlocked, so they let themselves in. "Hello!" Jane called out as they walked down the hallway. Almost immediately, the thundering of small feet was heard, and in a moment she was surrounded by little girls giving her hugs and crying out with happiness.

"I guess I was missed," she said with a smile to David. "Girls, this is Mr. Sheridan. He very kindly gave me a ride home. You probably recognize his name because his family so generously provides us with everything we need. Can we all welcome Mr. Sheridan?"

A chorus of voices rang out. "Welcome, Mr. Sheridan!"

Ruth asked Jane, "Did you fix the family emergency?"

"Everything is fine now," Jane assured her.

"Did you bring back our money?" asked Dorothy.

Sensing Jane's confusion, Mary interjected, "All of you will be repaid for the loan of your money plus interest, as promised."

David pulled out his wallet and produced a dollar bill. "Will this cover it?"

"No, sir, it's too much," Mary said. "The total was thirty-seven cents."

"Take it and use the rest to reward the girls' generosity." He put the bill into her hand and closed her fingers around it.

"Yes, sir. Thank you." She turned to the girls. "All of you will get your money back after the holidays. I have to go to the bank to get change."

David said, "If you don't mind, I'd like to use your telephone."

Mary took in a sharp breath. "I'm sorry, sir, but—"

"I know," he said, "there's a lock on it. I believe I can remove it. I need to call home and let them know my sister is still unaccounted for."

"I'll stay with the girls," Jane said. "Go ahead."

As they walked away, little Hazel wrapped her arms around Jane's waist. "Miss Shaw, I'm so happy you're home. Now you can tell us the Christmas story tonight!"

Home. The word warmed Jane's heart. Right now, there was no place she'd rather spend Christmas than here with all the girls. Jane nodded. "We'll sing Christmas carols, and before bedtime I'll tell you the Christmas story. It will be a real celebration."

Chapter Twenty-Nine

Jacquelyn's eyes adjusted to the darkness as the train lurched forward. The train car was empty except for the two of them and a few bales of hay. When Ezra had mentioned going to Milwaukee by train, she hadn't imagined she'd wind up in the same space used to transport farm animals.

"We're lucky that this was left behind," Ezra said, patting the hay next to him. "Sitting on the floor gets mighty cold, and standing gets mighty tiring."

Jacquelyn could see her breath, so as far as she was concerned it was already cold. She wasn't going to argue the point, though. She took a seat next to him and rubbed her mittened hands together. "Where does the train let out once it gets to Milwaukee?" Even sitting so close she had to speak loudly to be heard over the rhythmic sound of the train wheels moving down the tracks.

"The train yard is a good walk to downtown. I like to go past my daughter's house on the way to the rescue mission. Sometimes I can see them through the front window. I like that. Then I know that they're safe. After that, I'll have dinner at the mission. They put on quite a spread. It's a feast." He went on, listing all of the food that was offered on Christmas Eve and Christmas Day, but Jacquelyn's attention had been caught by an earlier detail.

"Your daughter lives in Milwaukee?"

"Yes, she does." He kneaded his forehead with his fingers like soothing a headache. "With her husband and two children."

"Why don't you spend Christmas with them?"

Ezra flapped a hand. "They wouldn't want me there. Don't blame 'em either. She has some bad memories of the olden days." He pulled a flask out of his knapsack and took a swig before offering it to her.

Gratefully, Jacquelyn accepted, but when she lifted it to her lips, she nearly choked. "You're drinking water?"

"You thought it would be something different?"

"Well, yes, I . . ." What was it that hobos were supposed to drink? "I thought it would be hooch."

"Hooch?" He threw back his head and laughed. "I guess I must look like a drinking man."

He wasn't wrong. She'd assumed as much from first sight. "No, I just thought a flask usually held whiskey or something like that."

Ezra leaned in toward her. "I'll tell you the truth. Right after my wife died, I used to drink my weight in the stuff. The local bootlegger was my best friend. Got liquored up on a regular basis. There are some parts of my life I can't remember, that's how bad it was. And then one day . . ." He had a thoughtful look on his face. "One day I decided I didn't want to live like that. Being in love with the bottle lost me everything—my money, my house, and all of my kinfolk. I knew it would kill me. So about five years ago I quit. I put it down and never picked it up again. It was hard, so hard. I'd get hungry for it and it would haunt my every thought, but I stood firm and I got through it."

"And that's why you say your daughter wouldn't want you there for Christmas?"

"Yes, that's why."

"It couldn't be as bad as all that."

"Oh yes, it could." His brow furrowed. "I hate to even think of all the things I've said and done."

"Have you tried talking to her? Apologizing?"

Ezra sighed. "No. Just too ashamed, I guess. One time I stood in the street and watched Delia and her family trimming the tree. They looked so happy. Me showing up would have ruined everything."

"You don't know that," Jacquelyn said, hugging herself. She swore the cold was creeping into her bones. "Maybe she would have been glad to see you. You could start fresh."

"No." He shook his head. "You'll find as you get older that sometimes it's just too late." He spoke with a finality that indicated the subject was closed. "Just too late."

Jacquelyn felt her stomach growl. The unfamiliar sensation reminded her of the food in Nellie's bag. She pulled out a square of brown paper and unwrapped it to reveal a sandwich brimming with meat and cheese, cut into two. Well, wasn't that nice? She couldn't believe Nellie had done this for a complete stranger, someone she wasn't likely to ever see again. People could be surprising. She held the sandwich out to Ezra. "Are you hungry? I'd be happy to split it with you."

"Don't mind if I do," he said, taking half. "Thank you."

They ate in companionable silence, washing down the meal with sips from Ezra's flask. Jacquelyn could never have imagined being in such a situation. Riding the rails with a hobo. It was like one of the radio serials that Mildred loved so much. In theory it sounded exciting, but instead it was a cold and uncomfortable way to travel. To think that this was Ezra's life. No home to speak of, just rambling around looking for a better place and the next meal. She shook her head. It couldn't be good for society to have citizens out and about without something productive to do. Someone really should do something to help these unfortunates.

Between the cold and the food, she found herself getting sleepy and nodding off. She awoke with a start when the train slowed, embarrassed to find she'd fallen asleep on the old man's shoulder. She sat up, rubbed her eyes, and yawned. "Are we in Milwaukee?"

"Yes, miss. Once we come to a stop, we'll need to get out right quick. Are you up to that?" He gave her a concerned look.

"Of course." It occurred to Jacquelyn that without Ezra she'd have no sense of direction and wouldn't know how to find her way home. Right now, in these circumstances, he was the best friend she could have.

When the train lurched to a halt, he went to the door and pulled it open partway, then stuck his head out to take a look. "The coast is clear," he told Jacquelyn, beckoning to the door. "Time to go."

He jumped down with surprising nimbleness, then extended a hand to help her exit the train car. When her boots hit the ground, she was alarmed to hear a man farther down the track yelling a stream of curse words aimed in their direction.

"Hurry!" Ezra yelled, taking off at a trot. Jacquelyn wasn't sure what would happen if that man caught up to them, but she didn't want to know. She ran.

Chapter Thirty

When David and Mary returned from Mrs. Irving's office, he had news for Jane. "I was able to remove the lock from the telephone." He then related his conversation with Mildred. "Eddie left to drop off the cookies, and she's made a point to guard the phone every minute since we've been gone. Still no word from Jacquelyn."

"I'm so sorry," Jane said, and she truly was. She felt responsible. Why had she agreed to switch clothing? Worse yet, why did she even get in the car? There'd been so many points at which she could have fixed this problem just by speaking up sooner, but she'd been too spineless to do so. "We'll have the girls pray for her safe return home."

"Thank you. I appreciate that."

Mary stepped forward. "Sir, are you going to return the lock to the telephone before you go?"

His brow furrowed. "I hadn't planned on it. In fact, I think you'll need to use it to call me if my sister comes back here. Why do you ask?"

"It's just that Mrs. Irving will be so angry with us if it's not the way she left it," Mary explained.

David gave her a comforting look. "Don't worry about that, Miss Howard. If Mrs. Irving has any objections, have her talk to me."

"Yes, sir." And then she added, "And please call me Mary."

"Very good, Mary."

Jane suppressed a smile. She'd never seen Mary look so smitten. David was nice and handsome, with movie star looks, so she understood the appeal. Still, to her mind, nothing about David compared to the inexplicable pull she felt for Eddie and his boyish charm. Even now she could recall his impish grin, as if he was letting her in on a secret. There was just something about him.

What David said next interrupted her thoughts. "If you could keep listening for the phone, I'd appreciate it. Call me immediately if you see or hear anything about Jacquelyn."

"I will," Mary said. "I'll go back right now and sit by the phone." She extended a hand toward David as if to shake. In return, he took it and gave her fingers a gentle squeeze. When she left the room, it was with a meaningful glance backward.

"I can't thank you enough," David said to Jane. "I'll call when we know where she is. And now I'd better drive back. I'll be watching for her along the way, of course. If she's not back by nightfall, I'm calling the police."

"I hope you find her safe and sound," Jane said.

"I do too," he said. "I'll be relieved once she's home, but part of me suspects that wherever she is, she's furious right now. She doesn't like it when things don't go her way. But if listening to her complain is the price for having her safely home, I'll gladly pay it." He pulled on his gloves. "As long as she's back and with us for Christmas, that's all that matters."

Chapter Thirty-One

Behind them the man screamed, "You two! Thieves! Come back here!" Jacquelyn had never heard anyone so angry. Was he really coming after them? And why? They'd done nothing wrong. The train car had been empty. It wasn't as if their presence made a difference either way.

Jacquelyn ran as quickly as she could, not looking back until the man's voice had receded in the distance. When they got a safe stretch away, Ezra slowed and waited for her to catch up. "That was a close one."

Out of breath, Jacquelyn managed to get out a few words. "What did he want?"

"To nab us, of course. I'm not sure what would have happened if he actually caught us. I don't think they would have thrown us in jail on Christmas Eve, but you never know."

"We could have been *arrested*?"

"Oh yes, miss. And a sad state of affairs that would have been. The food in jail is not nearly as good as at the mission, and there won't be any Christmas carols or special gingerbread cookies there neither." He clicked his tongue. "Nope, nothing good could have come of that."

"I'll keep that in mind." Her hand went to her side, pressing against the sharp pain made worse when she inhaled. "I think I hurt myself running. I might have broken a rib."

"You have a stitch in your side," Ezra said. How he knew that she had no idea. "It will go away. You just need to walk it off."

By this time, the train yard was far behind them. A row of houses to the right made her feel better. They were back to civilization. "Maybe someone here has a telephone I can use?" she asked hopefully.

He shook his head. "No one in this neighborhood can afford a phone. All the money they have is used for getting food on the table and keeping the lights on."

"Oh."

He led her through someone's yard to the street on the other side, then continued on. The houses here were like the ones she'd seen earlier when Eddie had driven her that morning. It was different seeing them while on foot.

At one of the houses, a woman came out to the front porch to shake a rug. "Merry Christmas!" she called out upon seeing them.

"Merry Christmas," Ezra said back with a wave.

"She seemed friendly," Jacquelyn said.

"Folks can be nice," Ezra agreed with a bob of his head. "Christmas brings out the best in people, I think."

They walked for what seemed like an hour, and then Ezra stopped so suddenly that Jacquelyn nearly walked right into him. "What?"

He raised one finger to point across the street. "That's Delia's house. The gray one with the dark roof."

"Your daughter's house?" Jacquelyn craned her neck to see. The house was better than most and actually had a Christmas wreath with a red bow on the front door. A picture window framed a decorated tree with a star on top on the other side of the glass. It looked as if reasonable people lived there. "Why don't we go up to the door and knock? If I explain who I am, it might help."

"No," he said, horrified. "I can't do that to her." He grabbed Jacquelyn's arm and pulled her forward. "Let's keep moving before she spots us."

Jacquelyn yanked her arm free from his grasp and kept walking. "It was just an idea. You don't need to manhandle me."

Ezra didn't respond until they were in the next block, and then he finally spoke. "I'm sorry." He sniffed and wiped his eyes.

"Are you crying?" Jacquelyn asked, fascinated. She'd never seen an adult man cry before. In her family, that would have been unheard of.

"My eyes get funny sometimes," he said ruefully. "It's just . . . sometimes I miss her so much. She was just the best little girl. I used to call her my sweetie pie. She thought the world of me then. That was before I ruined everything."

What did people say for this type of thing? Jacquelyn wasn't sure. "I'm sorry." That sounded right, for some reason, although what she could be sorry for she hadn't a clue. She'd only just met Ezra and wasn't even around back then.

He nodded in appreciation. "Thank you."

When they turned the corner several blocks ahead, it became evident they were entering the edge of downtown. Ezra said, "Not too much farther now. I can almost taste those gingerbread cookies. The line can get very long, but I think we'll be there in plenty of time to get a plate."

"Wonderful." Jacquelyn actually didn't plan to stand in any line for any length of time. She intended to find whoever was in charge at the rescue mission, reveal her true identity, and request—no, *demand*—that she be allowed to use their telephone. Her family donated substantial amounts of money to the rescue mission every year. They owed her.

When they arrived, Jacquelyn saw that Ezra was right. A line of people stretched thirty feet from the front of the building. It wasn't moving at all, but at least it was short. Ezra guided her to the back. On the way, he was greeted by some who were waiting.

"Ezra! You made it!"

"Welcome back."

"Merry Christmas!"

Sheepishly, he returned the words of welcome. "Thanks, gentlemen. It's good to be home."

Home. The word hit her like a gust of wind to the face. Odd that he considered this home.

The couple in line in front of them turned to talk to Ezra. Their skin was ruddy from the cold and their clothes ragged, but their smiles were wide. "Ezra!" the woman cried out, giving him a hug. "How was working at the Christmas tree farm?"

Ezra had a job? This was news to Jacquelyn, who'd assumed he'd gone north to beg for food. Of course, if she'd given it much thought, she would have realized he could have begged just as easily in the city.

"I liked it," he answered. "I slept in a barn with two other workers, and the food was good. The man paid me on time and said I can come back next year if I want."

She gave her husband a nudge. "You should have gone. Told ya."

"You know I could never leave you," he said. "I always say we don't have much, but at least we have each other."

Ezra said, "Where are you folks going to be staying for the holidays?"

"With Bertha's cousin for the rest of the month," the man said. "She invited us, even. Didn't have to ask. You?"

"I'll be sleeping here, same as usual." Ezra rubbed his hands together. "It will be good to get out of the cold."

"Excuse me," Jacquelyn said, stamping her feet to warm up. "I'm Jacquelyn Sheridan. Can you tell me how I can talk to the person in charge? It's very important."

"Oh, dearie," the woman said, "I don't think you'll be able to talk to anyone until you get inside." As if reading Jacquelyn's thoughts, she added, "And you can't skip ahead, or they'll ban you and send you packing. Happened to a friend of mine once."

They wouldn't dare, Jacquelyn thought, but still she stayed in place. She didn't want to spoil her chances of getting home. If she'd learned anything from the day's events it was that being dressed as Jane did her no favors. How could it be that a change of clothes gave her a different status? It hardly seemed fair.

And why did none of these people react to her name? It was as if her social position and money meant nothing to them. So puzzling.

Chapter Thirty-Two

EDDIE HAD DELIVERED HIS mother's cookies to the rescue mission for the last several years, so he knew to drop them off at the back door. His mother had packaged them in three white bakery boxes, the kind that held large sheet cakes, and filled them to the brim with gingerbread men.

The woman who came to the door had gray hair covered by a hairnet and a wide apron over her dress. She grinned when Eddie told her what he'd brought. "Wonderful!" she said, clapping her hands. "We get other bakery donations, but your mother's cookies are a favorite here. Tell her thank you from all of us. I can't even imagine how long it took her to bake and decorate this many. She's an angel here on earth."

"I'll let her know," Eddie said, handing them over. "Merry Christmas!"

"Merry Christmas to you too."

Getting behind the wheel of the Packard, he realized that he had absolutely no idea how long it had taken his mother to make the cookies. Couldn't even guess. It was just something she did every year, without fail. As reliable as the sun rising every morning. Everyone in the Sheridan household, including him, took her and her kindness for granted. He made a vow to be more heedful of the thoughtful deeds and charitable contributions she made everywhere she went.

Turning the corner of the building, Eddie saw the line of people, mostly men, forming down the block. *Poor souls.* Judging from the strained faces, they were tired and probably hungry. Some good food and Christmas cheer would make the day a little brighter for them.

Chapter Thirty-Three

JACQUELYN AND EZRA WERE still in line when she spotted a familiar vehicle going past. Her brother's Packard, with Eddie at the wheel. "Wait!" she screamed and took off running, moving through the slushy street faster than she would have even thought possible. Heart hammering, she felt her legs trembling, but she pushed through, watching as Eddie went through the intersection with nary a pause. When she saw the automobile stop at the next signed intersection, she yelled to two kids playing in their front yard. "Stop that Packard!"

One child regarded her blankly, while the other, an older boy, looked at the snowball in his hand and then deftly threw it right at the passenger-side window.

Jacquelyn crossed the street, yelling, "Eddie, Eddie!" as the automobile inched forward. As she got closer, the Packard came to a halt.

Upon glancing back and seeing Jacquelyn, Eddie's jaw dropped. He rolled down the window as she approached.

Through ragged breaths, she said, "Oh, thank goodness. For a minute there, I thought you were going to drive off without me."

He gave her a befuddled look. "Jane?"

She stared at him in disbelief. "No, you idiot, I'm Jacquelyn." Something was seriously wrong with him if he could be so easily fooled.

"Oh, Jacquelyn! I'm sorry. I was just surprised to see you."

She walked around and opened the front passenger door. Getting in, a wave of relief washed over her. This entire terrible experience was at its end. She was going home. "Thanks for leaving me behind," she said, an edge to her voice.

"You left specific instructions that Jane wasn't supposed to speak up until I noticed the difference. I didn't notice for a long time."

He made it sound like she'd brought the day's troubles upon herself. Upon reflection, she realized he wasn't completely wrong. Still, she wasn't going to admit it. "But I didn't think you'd leave me there."

Eddie gave her a smile. "But now you're here. Welcome back," he said. "Your brother is going to be so happy to hear you're safe and sound."

"And you aren't happy to see me?" She and Eddie had often been at odds, but surely he'd been concerned for her welfare? After all, he'd been the one to drive away without her.

"No, of course I'm happy to see you, but David has been frantic with worry."

"And you weren't." A statement, not a question.

"David and I saw your absence in a different light. He sees you as his little sister who needs protection, while I know that you're one of the strongest, most resourceful people I've ever met. I was sure you'd come out of this just fine and have a story to tell when all was said and done."

She straightened her posture. "If you must know, I made it all the way home using only my wits and the help of a few strangers."

"Impressive, but again, I'm not surprised. When you set your mind to something, there's no stopping you."

The Packard drove smoothly down the road, away from the city toward home. With a start, she realized that Eddie knew her better than she'd thought. She'd never paid much attention to him, but obviously, over the years, he'd taken notice of her. "You know that about me and still couldn't tell me apart from some stranger who works in the girls' home?"

He grinned. "I'm sorry about that. You do look nearly alike, it's true, but I should have looked beyond the clothing. Your personalities are very different."

"You like hers better?" Just a guess, but something in his expression made her wonder if she'd hit upon something true.

"Let's just say that your personality is perfect for you, and the same is true for Jane."

They spent the rest of the car ride in silence. Jacquelyn had so much she wanted to say, but she preferred to wait until David and Mildred were present. In the meantime, she was looking forward to being in her own warm house and eating some of Mildred's delicious food.

Chapter Thirty-Four

AFTER DINNER, ONE OF the older girls, Mabel, came to fetch Jane, saying, "The phone in Mrs. Irving's office is ringing!"

Jane hurried down the corridor, hoping and praying that the caller was David bringing the good news that his sister was home and safe. She wasn't sure if she could enjoy Christmas otherwise. She picked up the receiver and pressed it to her ear. "Sheridan Girls' Home, Jane speaking. How may I help you?"

"Jane!" A man's voice came through the earpiece. "Just the person I wanted to talk to. This is David Sheridan."

"Hello, Mr. Sheridan. You have good news, I hope?"

"I do indeed. My sister, Jacquelyn, is home and none the worse for all of her adventures."

Jane sank down into Mrs. Irving's chair. "Oh, I'm so glad!"

"She's already had a bath and a hot meal and regaled us with stories of her exceptional bravery." He chuckled. "No need to fear. Christmas is saved!"

Christmas is saved. It was as if he'd read her mind. "Thank the Lord," she said.

"I don't think she'll be switching lives with anyone ever again. It didn't quite turn out as she envisioned."

Jane understood. "The important thing is that she's safe and home."

As if the matter had been put to rest, he switched topics. "Did the girls enjoy the chocolates?"

"Mary and I decided to give them out after dinner, with the hot chocolate and story time. They don't know about the presents yet. I can only imagine the joy that will fill this building tomorrow morning at noon after we get back from church. Thank you again for paying for all of it. It was very kind of you."

"You're very welcome. Glad to help. We haven't shared the news about our shopping expedition with Jacquelyn just yet." She could imagine his smile as he spoke. "So she has no idea of her generosity. I think she's going to be very surprised."

She took in a breath. "I hope I didn't cause a problem for you."

"No, you didn't. I'm going to tell her that getting presents for the girls was my idea. Frankly, I've wanted to do it for years. And now that we've done it, it will continue."

Hand to her heart, Jane hoped it was true, or it would be a very sad Christmas next year. "Well, thank you again. You've made it a very Merry Christmas for all of us."

"Merry Christmas to you, Jane. Give my regards to Mary and the girls."

"I will."

After saying goodbye and hanging up, she remained in Mrs. Irving's chair reflecting on the day. How could so much have happened in so little time? Her life was back to the way it had been, and yet something was different. *She* was different. What a revelation to find out there was more out there than she'd ever imagined.

"Miss Shaw?" Mabel stood in the doorway. "Miss Howard said to tell you that she's ready to serve the hot chocolate."

"Thank you, Mabel. I'll be there in a minute."

When she got to the dining room, Jane saw that Mary and the girls had rearranged the tables to create a large space in the middle. The Christmas tree, still adorned with handmade ornaments, had been dragged into the room, taking a place of honor on one end. Mary had a large kettle of hot chocolate on a trivet on one table and was ladling it into mugs for the girls. "Be careful, it's hot!" she said repeatedly, as each one took her mug.

Once they were seated with their drinks in front of the tree, Jane retrieved the boxes of chocolates and brought them into the room. "Miss Howard and I have a surprise for you," she said, unwrapping the brown paper from the first box. "The Sheridans have kindly given us chocolates for our Christmas Eve celebration."

A murmur of excitement came over the group.

"Chocolate?" Frances cried out. "I love chocolate!"

"You've never even had chocolate," Ruth said, scoffing.

"Have so." Frances was indignant. "I've had chocolate lots of times."

"Hush, girls," Mary said. "Listen to Miss Shaw."

Jane explained that there was enough for each of them to have two pieces, and then she and Mary went around and let them select. For some, it was a lengthy, painstaking decision. "It's all delicious," Jane assured them. "You'll love whatever you pick."

When the girls were settled with their treats, Jane pulled out a chair in front. "Is everyone ready to hear the Christmas story?" she asked with a smile. Seeing all the nods, she began. "Long ago, in a town called Bethlehem, a baby boy was born . . ."

Chapter Thirty-Five

On Christmas morning, Jacquelyn woke early, quickly got dressed, and went downstairs. She found Mildred in the kitchen, frying bacon.

"Good morning, Jacquelyn," Mildred said with a bright smile. "I hope you're hungry. I'm making a feast for you and the boys."

Jacquelyn took a seat at the kitchen table. "Is there anything I can help with?"

Mildred turned and gave her a curious stare. "Are you feeling well?"

"Quite well. Why do you ask?"

"I don't know." Mildred shook her head. "Since you came back, you seem different is all."

"I feel different." Jacquelyn let the idea sink in. "Very different." Mostly, she was grateful to be home, but there was more to it than that.

"Very different, you say," Mildred repeated. "Good or bad?"

"Good, I think."

Mildred took her up on her offer to help, having her crack eggs into a bowl and stir them with a whisk. Jacquelyn had done this often as a little girl and remembered finding it satisfying. Why had she stopped? She couldn't recall.

The aroma of bacon lured David and Eddie to the room. Both were surprised to see Jacquelyn bustling around assisting Mildred, and they were even more startled when she suggested they all eat together in the kitchen, rather than separating the group with the Sheridans in the dining room and Mildred and Eddie in the kitchen.

While they were gathered around the table eating breakfast, Jacquelyn remarked, "It's awfully quiet here."

"Bet it's not quiet at the Sheridan Girls' Home," Eddie said with a grin. "Once Jane tells those girls about the presents, there's going to be a stampede."

"Presents?" She looked around the table. Eddie had a sudden guilty expression, while David looked like the cat that swallowed the canary.

"Oh yes, that," her brother said smoothly. "I've been meaning to tell you. While you were away yesterday, we purchased Christmas gifts for the girls at the home."

"You purchased gifts." She let that sink in for a moment. "Where did you buy them?"

"At Gimbels."

"I see." Everyone at the table was watching her to see her reaction. "And how many did you buy?"

"One for each, so fifty-two in all," David said. "We delivered them yesterday, but Miss Shaw is going to keep them hidden until after church this morning."

"Hmmm." She could tell that her reaction was making her brother nervous.

He said, "It was completely my idea. You know I've suggested doing it in the past."

She nodded. "I remember." Back then the girls at the home were nameless, faceless ingrates. Now that she'd met them, she could picture their sweet faces and feel their excitement at getting Christmas presents.

Eddie piped up. "So what do you think?"

"I think it's a splendid idea."

She saw relief wash over her brother's face. "You do?"

"Yes, I do. It's very nice of you. I wish I could see the girls when they get their gifts."

David said, "Actually, you could. If you'd like to drive up and be there when the gifts are handed out, it's entirely possible. We have plenty of time."

"If you're going, I'm going too," Eddie said.

"I'd so love to be there," Mildred said, pleading with hands together. "Please bring me along."

"Of course," Jacquelyn said. "All of us will go. When would we have to leave?"

"Ten thirty at the latest," David said, explaining the logistics of the trip and the plan for the presentation of the gifts to happen after church.

"Perfect," Jacquelyn said. "Then we have time to make one more visit before we go."

"Visit? What visit?"

"You'll see," she said, nodding to her brother. "After breakfast, bring the car around to the front. There's someone I have to meet, and I need you to drive me there."

Chapter Thirty-Six

David followed her from the automobile up to Delia's front door, still not sure why they were there. "Are these people expecting you?" he asked.

"Hush," Jacquelyn said. "You'll know soon enough." After she knocked on the door, they heard a flurry of activity inside. When the door opened, a little boy with wide eyes stood there wordlessly. "Can I speak to Delia, please?" she asked.

He turned. "Ma! There's a lady here wants to talk to you."

Delia came then, her hands rising to adjust her hair as she caught sight of Jacquelyn. "Yes, can I help you?"

"I hope so. I've recently made the acquaintance of your father, Ezra."

Her mouth dropped. "My father is still alive?" She clutched the doorframe. "How long ago did you see him?"

"Yesterday." She watched as Delia took in this news. "We had a long talk. He told me he quit drinking about five years ago and misses you, but he's too ashamed to come see you. He thought it was too late, that he'd ruined everything. He said when you were a little girl he used to call you—"

"Sweetie pie," she whispered, the blood draining from her face.

"Yes, that's what he told me."

"Where is he now?"

"He's at the rescue mission. Yesterday he came back into town after working at a Christmas tree farm north of here. I was stranded, and he kindly helped me find my way home." Jacquelyn was prepared to go on, to tell her how he'd shared his water and helped her get warm. That he'd been a perfect gentleman, despite his obviously disadvantaged circumstances. But before she could get the words out, Delia spoke up.

"I need to see him." She turned away and yelled into the house, "Earl! You won't believe it! This lady found my daddy." Tears were in her eyes when she turned back to Jacquelyn. "I've been praying for this day. Thank you so much."

"We'd be happy to drive you to the rescue mission," Jacquelyn said.

"No, my husband has an automobile," Delia said. "But thank you." She clutched a hand to her heart. "I'm sorry, I didn't get your name."

"I'm Jacquelyn."

"Thank you, Jacquelyn. Merry Christmas."

"Merry Christmas."

Back in the Packard, David said, "So that's the daughter of the hobo who helped you?"

Jacquelyn gave him a daggered look. "He's not a hobo. Just a man down on his luck. He has a daughter who loves him. And he owns a pocket watch, which he's never sold despite hard times. He's a good man."

"It was nice of you to help him."

"He helped me first."

David started up the engine. "And now we're heading home?"

"If you don't mind, I'd like to go to the rescue mission. Not go inside, you understand," she said, hurriedly. "I just want to wait."

"I understand."

When they arrived, David pulled the automobile to the side of the road where they had a good view of the front entrance. "So what exactly are we waiting for?" he asked after they'd been sitting there for a few minutes.

Jacquelyn craned her neck to get a better view. "Wait, I see them." As she watched, Delia and her family hurried down the sidewalk to the front door and went inside. Down the block, she heard the peal of church bells.

"I still don't understand," David said. "Why are we here?"

She turned to him. "Because I know most of the story, and I just have to see how it ends."

They sat in silence for fifteen minutes, the anticipation making Jacquelyn want to get out and go inside the building, but she held back, knowing she'd be intruding. Finally, her patience was rewarded by the sight of Delia's children coming out the door followed by who she assumed was her husband, Earl, who held the door for Ezra and Delia. Jacquelyn had seen Ezra smile before, memorably when she'd shared her sandwich, but his smile right now was something else. It stretched across his face in an expression of elation. This smile was the sun coming out from behind a cloud on a gloomy day. The smile of a man whose dearest wish, the one he couldn't have even hoped for, had just been granted. Delia too looked overjoyed.

"There they are." David said the words nonchalantly, as if this wasn't a miracle of the highest order. He had no idea the heartbreak that had just been mended. As the group turned the corner, he asked, "Are we done now?"

"We're done," Jacquelyn said with a nod. "Let's go home."

Chapter Thirty-Seven

DURING THE CHURCH SERVICE, all Jane could think about was how happy the girls would be when they handed out the presents. She was grateful that her young charges were on their best behavior in church, and when the choir sang "Silent Night," she felt the Christmas spirit fill her soul.

All of them felt it. During the long walk back, Mary led them in a rousing round of "Jingle Bells," and when one group mixed up their part, it led to laughter instead of the usual recriminations. Yes, it was a good day.

The night before, after the girls were in bed, she and Mary had made a plan. One of them would keep the group occupied while the other one moved the gifts from the storage room under the tree. When they let them into the room, it would be an incredible surprise. They'd debated what to tell the girls and ultimately decided to share that the presents had come from the Sheridans. Thank-you notes would need to be written, but that was a chore for another day.

She and Mary had had another topic of conversation the previous night. Mary had said, "Wouldn't it be wonderful if David Sheridan and Eddie came back one day and took us out to dinner?" Her tone had been giddy. "And maybe they'd fall in love with us and we could get married and have babies together!" Jane had agreed that this was a wonderful thought, but she knew it was just a dream. That kind of thing never happened to girls like them.

Once they'd arrived home from church, Mary made an announcement as they headed up the front drive. "I have an idea! We're going to have a snowman-building contest!" Jane slipped indoors, while Mary organized the impromptu competition. She shook off her wet outerwear and hung everything up to dry, then immediately went to the storage room.

She opened the door and blinked, her heart pounding in her chest. The presents that she'd seen neatly stacked in this very space the night before were gone. While they'd been away for that short time, someone had stolen their gifts. Her knees went weak, and she leaned against the doorframe to keep standing. No. That couldn't be. They'd never had problems with theft before. Why would this suddenly happen today of all days? The only logical explanation she could come up with was that Mrs. Irving had come back early, parked in back, and moved the gifts already. Unlikely, but possible.

She could only hope.

Jane hurried to the dining room, stunned to see Eddie, Mildred, David, and Jacquelyn standing in front of the tree, with all of the gifts on the floor behind them. "Surprise!" David said with a grin.

Eddie added, "All of us wanted to see the girls open their gifts."

"All of you wanted that?" Jane studied Jacquelyn's face for signs of anger, but there was none. Instead, she nodded.

"All of us felt that way."

Mildred pointed to a bag on the floor off to the side. "I laundered all your clothes and mended your dress too. You can barely see the rip."

"We'll get you a new dress as a replacement," Jacquelyn said hurriedly. "This is just for now."

Jacquelyn's demeanor was so different from what Jane had experienced before; it was as if she were a completely different person. Jane said, "Thank you." She took in a big breath. "I can't believe you made the long drive back for us."

Eddie said, "Personally, I wouldn't have missed it for the world." Again with a grin that made Jane's cheeks feel flushed.

"I guess I'd better go outside and get the girls, then," Jane said, awkwardly pointing behind her. "They're with Mary making snowmen. A sort of contest."

Chapter Thirty-Eight

EDDIE HAD BEEN RIGHT. The arrival of the girls coming into the room resembled a stampede. Jane only got them to settle down by threatening to take away the presents. Jacquelyn had the sense they all knew she'd never do it, but they weren't taking any chances. "We must be on our best behavior when guests are here," she said, introducing the four of them.

After they were seated cross-legged on the floor, Jacquelyn turned to Jane. "I'd like to hand out the gifts, if I may?"

"Of course."

One by one, she called out their names and they came up to claim their gifts. Jacquelyn said, "Don't open them until everyone has a present." Handing out fifty-two gifts took less time than she'd have thought. The girls were remarkably quick to claim their presents. When there was nothing more under the tree, she said, "Now you may open them up."

The older girls helped the younger ones with the string. The room filled with the sound of crinkling paper and the cries of the girls when they saw what they'd received.

"A doll! I've always wanted a doll."

"I got one too. Look at mine!"

"Oh, so pretty!"

"I love it."

Frances sighed and hugged her doll. "Christmas is the best time of the year."

Mary opened her box and immediately pulled on her gloves. "They fit perfectly. I feel like a high society lady." She looked toward the Sheridans. "Thank you so much."

Not one child acted disappointed, something that surprised Jacquelyn, who found her eyes inexplicably welling up with tears. She would have thought at least one girl would find another girl's gift to be preferable, but that wasn't the case at all. The room was full of gratitude and joy. When the girls quieted down, Jacquelyn called out, "I have another surprise for all of you."

"Another one?" Ruth said. "Oh boy!"

Jacquelyn said, "I think you'll like this one, Ruth. All of you will be getting pillows for your beds."

The room erupted in cheers. This time Jane didn't even try to quiet them.

"And," Jacquelyn continued over the din, "Miss Howard and Miss Shaw, who both work very hard to take care of all of you, will be getting raises." She nodded in their direction. "And you'll be able to access your own money for whatever you want or need."

As both Jane and Mary said their thanks, David leaned in toward her and whispered, "I don't recall the foundation approving these added expenditures."

"Oh, please. I think we both know who has the last word in these matters."

David threw back his head and laughed. "Now that's my sister. For a moment there, I thought I'd lost you."

"I'm not lost. I'm right here." She realized then that so much of her life had been spent in a state of discontent. She'd been busy casting about, flitting from one event to another, looking for something but never quite finding it. Who would have thought that on Christmas Day, in the dining room of the Sheridan Girls' Home, she would find herself right where she needed to be?

Chapter Thirty-Nine

WHILE EVERYONE ELSE WAS occupied, Eddie helped Jane pick up the discarded wrapping paper. "It's so pretty," she said, smoothing it out on the table. "We can use it again next year."

"Very resourceful," he said. "At the Sheridans', it goes right into the fireplace."

Jane shook her head in dismay. "We'd never do that. We don't throw out anything we can use."

"I've been wondering . . ." He hesitated for only a moment, and then his words came out in a rush. "I mean I was hoping I could write to you once I'm back at school. Are you allowed to get letters?"

Jane laughed. "Yes, I'm allowed to get letters. We get letters here all the time. I mean, all of us do, not just me." She hadn't meant to imply that she got letters from other young men. "I almost never get mail, except from my aunt maybe once or twice a year."

"I see."

"I would love to get a letter from you."

"Would you write me back?" He shifted nervously. "I know we haven't known each other for very long, but I enjoy your company and I feel like we get along. And I'd like to get to know you better."

"Of course I would write back." She wanted to say so much more, to let him know that she'd felt a spark of connection as well, but she found herself tongue-tied. "I would enjoy that very much."

"Can you have visitors?" he asked.

"Yes, I can have visitors on the weekend. I can even leave on outings as long as I get permission ahead of time." She couldn't remember the last time this had happened, though.

"You can leave?" His eyes widened in approval.

"Yes, I'm allowed to go anywhere I want as long as I'm back in time."

"Well, then, I'll write to you, and we'll make plans for an outing sometime in the future."

"I'd like that."

"It's a date," he said with a warm smile.

Jane felt a wellspring of happiness bubble up inside her. Funny how she'd thought yesterday had been the best day of her life. She'd had no idea it could get better.

Maybe things like this did happen to girls like her.

***

That evening, Jane finally had time to put away the clothing Mildred had so carefully mended and laundered for her. She hummed as she put it all away, and then she noticed a note card in the bottom of the bag.

Taking it out, she read:

Dear Jane,

I'm so glad we switched clothing yesterday. Doing so changed my life and opened my heart. As a wise little girl once said, Christmas truly is the best time of the year.

Gratefully,

Jacquelyn Sheridan

Jane read the message over and over again, running her fingers over the neat handwriting. She sent a thought out into the Christmas night: *The same to you, Miss Sheridan. The same to you.*

***

Thank you for reading *A Switch Before Christmas!* If you enjoyed the story, I'd be grateful if you'd consider giving it a rating or review.

Merry Christmas! Karen

***

More Christmas stories by Karen McQuestion

A TIME-TRAVEL CHRISTMAS

Christmas Eve 2022: When Elizabeth gets the news of her beloved grandmother's unexpected death, she's devastated. Heartbroken, she makes a wish on the brightest star in the night sky: *I wish I could see Grandma one more time.*

Christmas Eve 1957 : Ten-year-old Dodie is home caring for her sick little sister while her mother retrieves her father from the airport. At first all is fine, but as Betsy's fever spikes dangerously high, a terrible snowstorm knocks out the power and phone. With her parents long overdue and Betsy nonresponsive, Dodie begins to panic. In the midst of this crisis, a woman comes to the door saying she's lost. She seems vaguely familiar, and Dodie needs the help, so despite everything she's heard about strangers, she opens the door and lets her in...

***

WISH UPON A CHRISTMAS STAR

When Gwen Hayward moves to the quaint town of Poplar Creek, she's too mired in post-divorce misery to meet the neighbors. That changes when she spots a little girl leave an anonymous wish on the local bookstore's Christmas tree. Compelled to find the girl and fulfill the wish, Gwen enlists the aid of local business owner, Lucky Gallagher.

With the help of the townspeople, a lost dog, and some holiday magic, Gwen and Lucky may see more than one Christmas wish come true.

About the author

Karen McQuestion has written more than twenty-five books for all ages. Christmas stories are particular favorites of hers. She's written three so far and has ideas for more. She lives in Hartland, Wisconsin.

Acknowledgements

The first person who read this story is the first one I'd like to thank. My gratitude to my friend, MaryAnn Schaefer. You made some great catches and also gave me much needed validation. It wasn't a book until you told me it was a book.

Thank you also to my sons, Charlie and Jack. Each of you proved to be an excellent proofreader. Jack excelled at finding anachronisms, while Charlie's comments made me laugh. Both of them found things I missed.

I have the best family. Loving and supportive, and always there for me. I wake up in gratitude every single day.

To Jessica Fogleman who took on this editing job and helped shape the story in so many ways. Thank you, Jessica! You have an eagle eye and a kind way about you. I'm grateful for your expertise and I loved reading your notes.

Lastly, I'd like to thank you, whoever you are, for taking the time to read this story. It means the world to me.

www.ingramcontent.com/pod-product-compliance
Lightning Source LLC
Chambersburg PA
CBHW060452300726
48975CB00008B/2486